THE GREAT AMERICAN SONGBOOK

THE GREAT

AMERICAN

S O NG

B O OK

STORIES

BY SAM ALLINGHAM

A
STRANGE
OBJECT
Austin, Texas

The stories in this collection have appeared in slightly different form in the following publications:

"Rodgers and Hart" in *American Short Fiction*, "Stockholm Syndrome" in *Epoch*, "Love Goes to a Building on Fire" in *The Coffin Factory* (as "The Way Love Sinks"), "One Hundred Characters" in *Web Conjunctions*, "Assassins" in *No Tokens*, "Tiny Cities Made of Ashes" in *StoryQuarterly*, "Bar Joke, Arizona" in *One Story*, and "The Great American Songbook" in *The Atlas Review* (as "Songs").

Published by
A Strange Object
astrangeobject.com

ISBN 978-0-9892759-9-6

Cover design by Natalya Balnova
Book design by Amber Morena

to L.P.
you're the one for me

CONTENTS

SHEET MUSIC

Brother Grant heard supernatural beings singing a song
one night, AMERICA HAS FORGOTTEN GOD. He awoke
and wrote the song down. Now, he has it in sheet music.
It sells for 90 cents. If you order it this month and request
it, he will send you a beautiful bottle of pure olive oil
from an old olive tree in Jerusalem. You can use this
anointing oil for years to come.

—KEITH WALDROP, *Light While There Is Light*

RODGERS AND HART
\\\\\\\\

Morning

When Rodgers opens his door to go to work, the weather is clear and the air is fragrant with honeysuckle. The bees swoop in melodic arcs, the birds call in mellifluous harmony, and the trolley cars trundle in metered time.

When Hart steps outside, it is raining. Cockroaches wave their greedy legs, the crows call, the taxicabs bleat impatiently. The wind blows his hat across the street, where it lands on the head of a stockbroker.

Faces

Rodgers is often photographed. His eyes look like painted irises.

Hart is rarely photographed. Every part of his face is a half inch too large.

The Theater

Rodgers loves the theater. He likes the bustle, the chatter, the occasional hammer-fall of a carelessly struck piano—the 365 components resonating in a well-assembled hum.

Hart does not like the word *theater*. It is very difficult to rhyme.

Styles of Dress

Hart's manner of dress is quite variable. Sometimes he will show up for rehearsal in a crisp, tailored pinstripe suit. Other times he will show up in his soiled shirtsleeves with a black eye. Once, during the rehearsals for *Pal Joey,* he showed up in a Hungarian soldier's outfit, terribly wan, and whispered in Rodgers's ear: "I haf come to suck your blaad."

Rodgers owns twenty versions of the same gray suit.

Manners of Speech

Rodgers is a fluid speaker. His words have a musical quality, in that they are light as air, spoken and then forgotten.

Hart talks slowly.

The Piano

Playing the piano is Rodgers's favorite pastime. While playing the piano, Rodgers often loses track of time. He forgets to eat, drink, and sleep.

While Rodgers plays the piano, Hart tries in vain to attract his attention. He dances clumsily. He makes horrific faces. He weeps in silence.

When Rodgers is not around, Hart bangs his fat and clumsy fingers against the keys.

Once, Rodgers tried to buy Hart a piano. It was not a success.

Punctuality

Hart is never punctual and always apologetic.

Rodgers is never apologetic and always punctual.

Expressions

Rodgers's favorite expression is "all right."

Hart's favorite expression is "all right."

Living Situations

Hart's apartment is fantastically dirty. Clothes, papers, and cigarette ash accrue in layers, so that one could almost make a geological survey of his personal habits.

Rodgers's apartment is immaculate. He is almost never there.

Methods

Rodgers tells his students: "One note leads to another." He loves to describe his methods.

Hart tells his drinking companions: "One word hides another." He claims to have no methods.

Editing

Hart's lyrics take a long time, like children, and are sometimes rejected.

Rodgers's melodies appear instantaneously, like sunbeams, and are always appreciated.

Parents

Hart's parents are poor Jewish immigrants who speak Yiddish. He has a hard time speaking to them.

Rodgers's parents are wealthy, assimilated Jews who speak proper English. He has a hard time speaking to them.

How They Met

Hart met Rodgers at a music hall mixer at Columbia University. He asked Rodgers if he knew the tune to "High Society." Rodgers did not respond. He couldn't hear what Hart was saying. The ballroom was loud, and Hart talked with his hand over his mouth. Rodgers did not remember him.

Rodgers met Hart when he came across the other man sitting alone in a recital room, clumsily stringing together a facsimile of "High Society," flatting and sharping crucial notes.

"Let me show you how to do it," Rodgers said, alighting gracefully on the piano bench.

Men

Rodgers barely notices them, except as voices.

Hart always notices them.

Rodgers on Hart

Publicly, Rodgers calls Hart a genius, a wordsmith, a first-rate poet, a sophisticate, an aesthete, a top-notch ironist, a man with flair, the Bard of Manhattan.

Privately, Rodgers calls Hart a drunk, a spendthrift, a lout, a lazybones, a pervert, a washout, a gigantic waste of talent.

Hart on Rodgers

Publicly, Hart calls Rodgers an arrogant louse, a prig, a snob, Mr. Uptight, Park Avenue Princess, the Icebox, Madam Milquetoast, Stoneface, the Rajah of 102nd Street, and Toodles the Composing Chimpanzee.

Privately, Hart talks endlessly of Rodgers's graceful fingers.

Drinking

Rodgers is too busy laughing and shaking the hands of new acquaintances to drink.

Hart is never too busy.

Love

As a composer, Rodgers defines love in three varieties: young love, an upward leap from the tonic to the fifth, something like a round horn calling from a hilltop; unrequited love, a major chord melting into an unexpected minor tone like ringing glass; and contented love, the clean interval between the third and the fifth, sometimes rising to the major sixth and twinkling like a round, white star.

As a lyricist, Hart thinks of love as a dumb bear he must force to dance.

Childhood

When Hart was a child, he wrote a poem, and his mother couldn't read it.

When Rodgers was a child, he wrote a song, and his mother signed him up for piano lessons.

The Police

Hart spends a great deal of time in the police station, but nobody remembers his face.

Rodgers only comes down to the police station to pick up Hart, but the patrolmen brag about meeting him for days afterward.

Troubles

Hart has many troubles, including, but not limited to: money trouble, love trouble, heart trouble, stomach trouble, pitch trouble, ear trouble, family trouble, nose trouble, lung trouble, wart trouble, hair trouble, house trouble, and trouble with the police.

When Rodgers has trouble, he immediately begins to whistle "Wrap Your Troubles in Dreams," and the trouble disappears.

The Break

The last words Hart says to Rodgers are: "You've taken advantage of me."

The last words Rodgers says to Hart are: "You're so glad to be unhappy."

Where They Are

Everyone always knows where Rodgers is.

Nobody ever knows where Hart is.

Farewell

On the eve of his death, Hart writes a long good-bye letter to Rodgers. He never sends the letter. It is later found on the floor of his apartment, shuffled and sorted among lost lyrics, cries of pain and woe, horse-track betting forms, past-due utility bills, profiles of silent movie stars, and lists of dubious snake-oil stomach remedies.

By the time Rodgers receives the letter, he is already hard at work on another musical. Upon reading Hart's words, he immediately composes a song in which he trans-figures the first line of each paragraph into a series of me-lodic fragments. After he is done writing the fragments, he throws the letter away.

The tune—somewhat revised—later appears as a love song in the musical *Me and Juliet*, which is not a success.

Ghosts

Near the end of his life, Rodgers admits to his few close friends that he has been haunted for a number of years by the ghost of Hart, who appears while Rodgers is compos-ing, leaning on the side of the piano and staring at his fin-gers. Hart looks terrible in death; his mouth hangs open in an expression of yawning sadness. The only way to get him to leave is to stop playing the piano.

After his death, Rodgers never haunts anyone.

STOCKHOLM SYNDROME
\\\\\\\\\

EVERY SUNDAY A COUPLE COMES INTO the coffee shop where Betty works. The man is tall, wrapped in a thin khaki jacket, and wears dark sunglasses. The woman— his wife, Betty assumes—is much smaller, with tight, dark ringlets and heavy makeup. The woman leads the man by the hand. The man walks unsteadily; Betty wonders if he is blind or has some kind of mental illness.

"Two lattes, one skim and one whole," the woman says.

She always orders the same thing.

The man never says anything. His head turns this way and that, as if taking in the whole of the shop, but to Betty it doesn't seem as if he sees anything. This is why

9

she wonders if he is blind; she's seen blind people do the same thing, turning their heads as if they're able to feel the size of the room with their faces. His wrinkled, leathery face has a couple of large, white scars.

Other people who work at the café find the couple endearing. Valerie, who works Wednesday mornings, says that they have renewed her faith in romance.

"I hope somebody takes care of me like that when I'm old," Valerie says.

Valerie's boyfriend is a guitar player who does odd jobs at the Methodist Ministries Homeless Center. He comes in sometimes around noon, having just woken up, and smiles at everybody in a hazy way. Betty notices the way that Valerie loses focus whenever he's around, the way that her line of sight bends toward him as he makes his shuffling way around the shop.

"That's love," Valerie says, looking at the blind man's wife rubbing his hands. "Somebody to warm your hands up in the morning."

When someone makes these kinds of comments about the blind man and his companion, it makes Betty feel a little ill. It's not that she doesn't like the couple, per se. They've never been anything but polite to everyone on staff. But she doesn't like to think of them as an ideal, as something people would aspire to, this shuffling man wandering behind his wife. She doesn't like the slow way they walk through the door together.

Then, one day, the woman gets the order wrong. Betty is working the register.

"Two lattes," the woman says.

"Whole or skim?" Betty asks.

"Whole," the woman says.

She seems distracted, a little tense. She bunches her fingers up on the counter.

Betty knows that this is wrong. She almost prompts the woman—*you meant skim for the second one, right*? But it's not her business, and she makes both lattes the same.

A few minutes later, Betty hears angry mutterings from the far booth.

"Do you expect me to drink this?"

The man scowls at his wife.

"Why don't you just *give* me a heart attack?" he says.

"I'll get you another one, Tom."

The woman looks at the ceiling. Her lip shakes a bit.

"Why can't you do anything right?"

Betty is shocked by how angry the man sounds. She has always assumed that blind people are inherently kind and considerate—and now, hearing the tight, hissing sound of his voice, she realizes how naïve this is.

"I'm sorry," the woman says to the man. "I just wasn't thinking."

The man doesn't say anything.

The woman comes back to the counter and gives Betty an embarrassed smile. Betty notices that she is breathing heavily.

"I'm sorry," she says. "I made a mistake. I need a skim latte."

"My mistake," Betty says. "I'll make you another one—I'll drink this one."

The woman smiles.

"Thank you so much," she says.

"Don't mention it," Betty says. She feels sorry for the woman.

Later, as she's leaning against the counter in a slow period, she looks across the room at the couple. She sees the woman reach up and run her fingers lovingly over the blind man's forehead, taking two fingers and stroking the fine lines of a scar. The whole while the man just sits there impassively, like a statue.

She tries to tell Thomas about this when he comes in for the evening shift.

"He was so cruel about it," she says. "I couldn't believe it."

"You never know what it's like inside a relationship," Thomas tells her. "It's a closed system. Think about it: those people have had years together—they've been butting up against each other, going back and forth. It's not logical."

"A closed system," Betty repeats. "That sounds very technical."

"It is technical," Thomas says, and laughs.

They wipe down the counters in uneasy silence. She watches the light filter through Thomas's thin beard. She would describe him as her closest friend at the shop, but there are still a number of things they don't talk about. Thomas is so giving in conversation that it's easy for her to gloss over the things she would rather avoid.

Betty has a hard time thinking positively about relationships these days. She has to stop herself from imagining the most negative associations. When Thomas tells her that relationships are a closed system, she thinks immediately: Stockholm syndrome. When you're closed off from the outside world, you start to take on the worldview of your captor. Their voice echoes in your head, and you see all things through their eyes.

ACCORDING TO BETTY'S READING—she's become a big reader, now that she lives alone—the original case of Stockholm syndrome took place during the Norrmalmstorg robbery of the Kreditbanken in Stockholm. The robber, a man named Jan-Erik Olsson was attractive in a wild sort of way, and the hostages bonded strongly with him, taking his side in negotiations with the police. Even after being freed by the authorities, the hostages corresponded with Olsson for many years while he was in prison. They even petitioned the authorities to commute his sentence.

It wasn't only the hostages who were enamored with Olsson. During his stay in prison, he received mail from hundreds of women. Many of them expressed their admiration and sympathy for him. Others expressed emotional identification and physical attraction. Some of these letters had to be heavily edited by the prison censors. Other prisoners referred to the women Olsson corresponded with as the "rånare harem," or "robber's harem."

And Betty had come across a picture of the hostages—two beautiful women who looked to be in their mid-twenties—during their captivity. Olsson stood over them with a dour expression. The hostages stood next to the security vault with nooses around their necks. She was horrified by the picture, but underneath it she read a quote by one of the hostages: "We were trying not to laugh. We were all in on the stunt. We wanted to help Jan escape by making the police think he was serious. We were all on the same team."

Maybe that's love, Betty wonders: a spell that never breaks. She wonders the same thing when she sees Valerie mooning over her guitarist boyfriend, who never says anything other than a muffled hello, whose smile is so gauzy you can see through it. She wonders the same thing when the woman with the ringlets comes in, leading her blind husband. If the spell never breaks, you never notice anything is wrong. Now, when she sees couples together, sitting in silence in the shop or walking down the street with their hands clasped together and their eyes forward, she imagines a bubble surrounding them, insulating them from the outside world. It sits between her and them, refracting what they see.

VALERIE WANTS TO KNOW if Betty is an introvert or an extrovert. She's always asking these sorts of questions. She also wants Betty to take a Myers-Briggs personality test, so as to better figure out the kind of people she might be attracted to.

"I'm intuitive," Valerie says. "If you're intuitive, it's very important to be with someone else who is also intuitive. Otherwise you just won't fit together emotionally. That's the number one most important aspect of the test for relationships."

Betty thinks to ask whether Valerie's guitar player boyfriend is intuitive, but she knows that if she starts with it, Valerie won't be able to stop. So she makes a double mocha and lets it alone.

Thomas is an extrovert. That much Betty can figure out without having to ask. All of the people who come into the shop seem to like Thomas. If he calls in sick—which he does fairly often, to take care of his girlfriend, who has some sort of mysterious illness—they ask about him. *And where's Thomas this fine afternoon?* Betty gets the impression that the customers, especially the women, look forward to seeing Thomas as part of their daily routine, and that seeing him may be more important to some of them than the coffee they order out of social necessity—and certainly Thomas enjoys their company, calling out their names the minute they walk in the door, asking after their children and grandchildren. He sometimes holds up the line, just to bask in their appreciation, but no one seems to begrudge him this. The customers wait patiently for their turn in the sun.

It was this friendliness and openness that Betty liked about Thomas in the first place. Before she got the barista job, she had gone through a dark period, and when she and Thomas began working together, the steady hum of conversation between Thomas and all the regulars, along with the warm light through the open front window, made it feel as if heavy clouds were lifting at last. Sometimes, stacking chairs when the evening shift was over, listening to Thomas making gentle fun of one regular or another, she would imagine various possibilities—and he was always kind enough to walk her to the bus stop and wait in the dark until it arrived.

ONE SUNDAY IN THE PUBLIC LIBRARY, Betty stumbles across this textbook definition: *Stockholm syndrome is difficult to diagnose, because the perspective most useful in defining it—the victim's—is also the least reliable. For instance, one of the most important factors in identifying Stockholm syndrome is the threat of physical violence, but many victims steadfastly deny any violent behavior in their captors, despite all evidence to the contrary.*

Betty knows this to be true. She remembers an ache in her scalp, a twisted shoulder. She remembers thinking, *I must be sitting too long at work; I must be lying on my hair wrong after a shower*—anything but the most obvious explanation.

She thinks of this as she reads about Frances Eberhardt, famous victim of Stockholm syndrome: a young woman who was found wandering around at a gas station near Spokane, Washington, with bruises on her legs and arms, suffering from borderline starvation. She was waiting for her husband to come back, she said, and refused to say anything else, even after the authorities discovered the body of a young woman near the gas station, later identified as Giselle Eberhardt, her daughter. Semen samples and fingerprints matched a man currently being held on burglary charges forty miles away, in Wattakua: a man named Gerald Hoffstra, who happened to be Frances Eberhardt's husband.

When the authorities reunited husband and wife, Frances Eberhardt collapsed in his arms, and when the case of her daughter's murder came to trial, she gave confused and conflicted evidence on the stand, as if she were actively trying to cover up her husband's whereabouts on the day of the murder and provide him with an alibi.

The police later determined that Frances Eberhardt had been abducted by Gerald Hoffstra at the age of nineteen, along with her infant daughter. They hypothesized that he had been abusive almost from the start, controlling her eating habits and confining her to his car if she "misbehaved." The authorities also maintained that he had been sexually abusive and that he later repeated these habits with her daughter. Despite this, Frances Eberhardt testified to his innocence up to the point of execution and afterwards wrote frequent letters to the editor of the small Spokane newspaper, proclaiming his innocence and petitioning the state to get rid of the death penalty entirely. "I am all alone in this world," she wrote, in one such letter. "And for this I have only the government of Washington to blame."

Betty shivers when she reads the words "Spokane, Washington." It makes her remember her boyfriend Will and the first leg of their cross-country trip together, from Seattle to Philadelphia—how a sign for Spokane, Washington, rose up to meet them and then receded in their wake.

"Good riddance," Will said. "Good riddance to this whole fucking coast."

"Right," she said. She was trying to stay buoyant. "Onward to the future!"

He reached his hand over and cupped her knee, and

she felt the surety of the road stretching out in front of her. She had made a few good friends in Seattle, but Will hadn't liked them. They had said strangely suspicious things about him that had made her feel uneasy. In Philadelphia, she told herself, things would be different.

But then there was the rest stop, just after they crossed into Idaho. When they passed through the double doors and passed the crane machine to Roy Rogers, he grabbed her arm and held her close, as if he was afraid of losing her—as if she might disappear into the crowd and leave him behind. She remembers wanting to whisper, *You don't need to hold so tight*. He looked so sad in those days, pale and skinny in his Smiths T-shirt. You could see in his eyes this overwhelming need for love.

When she went to pay, she found that her wallet was missing.

"You dropped it on the floor of the car," he spoke from behind her shoulder. "Lucky I picked it up."

He took out her money and paid for them both.

It's good I have Will around to remember things, she often told people. *I'm so absent-minded*.

BETTY DOESN'T REALLY KNOW Thomas's girlfriend, Leigh Anne. Nobody at the shop does. She never comes in; when she does come to meet Thomas, she calls in advance and has him meet her in a health food store a few blocks away, where Thomas says she buys her tinctures and herbal supplements. Leigh Anne has a number of health problems that Thomas can never quite explain, problems that make it difficult for her to get out of bed in the morning.

"It's sweet of Thomas to take care of Leigh Anne like that," Valerie says. "A lot of people would have let somebody like that drop."

"That's true," Betty says.

"I mean, Thomas is so sensitive. Feeling/Intuitive, like I said. It's the most important thing."

Betty nods. She knows she should be more considerate to Valerie—maybe it's her snobbishness that makes it hard for her to strike up friendships—but so much of what she says seems clichéd.

"But you have to think that it's way hard for him," Valerie continues. "I don't feel like he gets out much."

Once, when Betty was near the end of a shift, a man came into the shop with a guitar on his back. Betty recognized him as one of the instructors from the guitar shop across the street. He was the only customer in the shop, and Thomas leaned across the divider and asked him a few questions.

"I only know the basic chords," Thomas said. "Do you think I'd be able to muddle through the harder ones if I just got myself a book?"

"Oh, I'd give you cheap lessons," the man said. "I'd give you the friend discount."

As Betty turned the sign to Closed, Thomas went around the counter and pulled the guitar out of its case. It was a beautiful instrument—despite Betty's lack of understanding, she could tell it was expensive—and Thomas handled it very gently, propping it on his knee and strumming a few chords. The sound reverberated off the polished floor.

Thomas began to sing and play, an old folk song Betty remembered from a movie she had seen once. His voice wasn't well trained—it slipped around a few of the notes—but it had a warm tone to it that matched the rest of Thomas's personality. He sang for a few minutes, with the guitar teacher looking on appreciatively, and then his phone rang. He passed the guitar back to the teacher with a worried look and rushed to answer it.

"Yes," he said, whispering softly into the phone. "I'm sorry. I'll be out in a minute."

After he hung up he turned to Betty.

"Can I trust you to close up shop?"

Betty nodded, and in ten minutes he was gone, off to take care of Leigh Anne and her mysterious sickness.

How many times has she closed up alone as a favor for Thomas? She's lost count. Leigh Anne calls—Betty can hear the panic in her voice, even on the other end of the line—and then Thomas has to go, a puppet on strings.

She only gets hints of Thomas's secret life—once it was guitar playing, and once it was a poem he was working on in the back, when things were particularly slow on a Sunday. She always expects more than she gets, and when she sees it, it's gone in a second—a customer interrupts or he gets an emergency phone call.

When Betty and Thomas began working together, Betty always thought they would spend time together, eventually, outside of the shop. She figured that one day Thomas would lean the broom in the closet, wipe his hands on a rag, and ask her if she would like to come over to his apartment for a drink. But they have known each other for a year now, and this has never happened.

"It's been such a relief having you around," he tells her, one night at the bus stop when the bus is delayed. "Nothing against Valerie, you know—but you get tired of the same conversation, over and over. It's nice to work with someone you can really talk to."

It's no revelation; anybody would be bored, stuck with Valerie shift after shift. But it suggests that Thomas looks forward to their conversations, too—that it isn't just Betty imagining things, as she has so often in the past.

But then the bus arrives, and she gets on without a word. Thomas goes home to Leigh Anne.

IN COLLEGE, BETTY WROTE her undergraduate thesis on the poet Catherine Tierney. Betty's advisor, who wanted to groom her for life as an academic, felt that Tierney was too minor a figure to merit such close attention, her *Collected Poems* barely large enough to qualify as a book. But Betty was sympathetic to Tierney, married to Walker Burdon, the son of a rich industrialist who suffered from a nervous disorder; she spent her life traveling to various centers and retreats throughout Europe, tending to her husband's needs. No wonder she had little time to devote to her own work.

Betty wonders now why she was so drawn to Tierney's work. Her thesis was about "the metaphysical nature of love"; she remembers reading the lines "in this close space we break together / open and outward, tunneling in" as an expression of desire. She remembers reading it to Will when they were both undergrads, before he dropped out because he couldn't get along with any professors—the way he nodded solemnly, as if it expressed their relationship perfectly. He didn't care much for poetry, except in songs, but he understood how love should be: all-consuming, two souls coming together.

Betty's thesis did not mention the most recent, controversial biography of Tierney, the one that focused on her relationship with Burdon and suggested it was emotionally and physically abusive. During a stay in a private resort in Priano, Italy, for example, the writer claimed that Burdon trapped Tierney in a broom closet and beat her viciously with a cane. Perhaps there were other reasons her advisor warned her to focus on someone else, other than Tierney's contemporary reputation.

And yet Betty was still reading Tierney after she and Will moved to Philadelphia, after her academic career seemed like a dream from another life, after Will's behavior began to grow worse, impossible to ignore. *In this close space*: the way he began waiting up for her every evening at home, furious that she'd been out too long, grabbing her arm and pulling her inside, away from prying eyes. *We break together*: the beer bottle that flew past her head and shattered on the far wall, after she wore down the batteries for the DVD remote and ruined his evening.

LATER SHE TOLD HERSELF, *He didn't throw it at my head. He didn't want to hit me.*

Later she told herself, *He was aiming for the wall, I think*.

Later she thought, Why did I say this? Who was I trying to convince? There was no arguing with the sound of the bottle, parting the air around her ear, or the sound of a fist moving through space, seeking soft flesh to cushion the blow.

Open and outward: the way Will would smile when they were in public, the way he would feed her pineapple on the riverside promenade and then whisper in her ear, "Aren't you happy? Aren't I good to you?" She would see them as she thought they looked from the outside: a happy young couple, college-educated and beautiful, impervious to harm. She would forget that Will had never graduated, that he lived off the money his parents sent every month, that he resented her for finishing. *You could get along with those assholes*, he told her. *You've always been good at pretending to like people*.

Tunneling in: his hand on her arm, tight, fingers gathered in her hair, pulling hard at the roots, bodies slamming together as she'd come to think she liked, or at least deserved. His mouth near her ear, a trembling, desperate tongue repeating, *Tell me you like it*. He was digging into her, deeper by the day, looking for safety, until they were the same; she was the aider and abettor of all his crimes. She would build a wall around his anger with her body, to protect him from himself.

Sometimes, after she moved out of that apartment and issued a restraining order against him, she would be coming home to her new place, hear footsteps behind her, and wonder if it was Will following her. She would be frightened at first, but when she got home, the fact that he hadn't followed her, that she hadn't told him where she lived, and that, if the police had their way, she would never see him again would hit her in full, and it would take all of her willpower to avoid picking up the phone and calling him.

She was lonely. It was still winter, and she had a hard time making close friends. That was how powerful the spell was, but in the end she broke it. She got a new job, in a new neighborhood. She took her *Collected Poems of Catherine Tierney* and burned it in the backyard.

Now she tries her best to remember that she is whole on her own. She takes long walks in the neighborhood around the shop, hoping to run into someone she knows and strike up a conversation, but when someone she has seen before comes walking up to her, she only smiles politely and keeps walking. She can act the role of the kind neighbor, but what would she do if she lost the script; how could she explain the last three years of her life? Her weakness is unspeakable, a list of crimes too strange to explain. They would be horrified to hear the truth.

She must move forward in tiny steps, so small that others might not notice them at all. She counts the little victories: a kind conversation in passing, someone calling her name. Thomas lives in the neighborhood; sometimes she walks by his window to see if his light is on.

THEN, ONE DAY, WHEN THE WEATHER is warm and the babies are all cooing in their strollers, the thing Betty has pretty much given up expecting finally happens:

Thomas asks her if she would like to come over to his apartment for dinner the next evening.

"We'll get a chance to talk," Thomas says. "It's so busy here, we never get a chance to have a real conversation like I'd like."

"Right," Betty says. "I mean, me too."

Betty tries to stay subdued. The last thing she wants is to ruin a new friendship by being too eager.

She works the morning shift the next day, which gives her three empty hours between the end of work and Thomas's invitation. She walks around Washington Square Park, sits for a while on a bench, but has a difficult time concentrating on the book she's bought. In the liquor store she ponders whether she should bring a white or a red wine.

At six she rings the doorbell. She's worried—was the wine too much? She reminds herself that friends bring wine; it doesn't mean anything.

Thomas comes down to meet her.

"I'm so glad you could come," he says. "And you brought wine!"

He has such a way of making people feel appreciated. Betty finds herself smiling widely.

He has already prepared a summer meal—quinoa and black bean salad, some asparagus with fennel, laid out in such flimsy plastic bowls that Betty finds it endearing, the combination of culinary expertise and slipshod presentation, as if he doesn't quite know how good he is at what he does. But isn't that Thomas's charm, she thinks, this unknowing goodness? And the food is very good—she has to remind herself to slow down.

They drink and talk about work, the various crazies that come in. Talk turns to the woman and her blind husband.

"Do you want to hear something crazy?" Thomas asks. "Sometimes I wonder if he did it to himself."

"What?" Betty tries to appear incredulous, as if she hasn't imagined such strange scenarios around the couple before. "You mean plucked out his eyes?"

"Or acid, or something," Thomas says. "Just to keep her around. It would be totally Flannery O'Connor."

Finally, in a lull in conversation, Betty puts her chin in her hand and cocks her head inquisitively.

"Where's Leigh Anne tonight?"

"Oh, she's here," Thomas says, lowering his voice. "That reminds me, we shouldn't be too loud. She's been feeling weak lately, so she's resting in the back room."

"We could save her some wine," Betty says, and then puts her hand over her mouth, realizing that maybe she's gone too far.

Thomas smiles a half smile.

"That's a good joke," he says sadly, as if remembering a time before Leigh Anne got sick, when she might have joined their party.

He looks unhappy all of a sudden, and for the first time, Betty thinks she notices cracks in his mask. So he knows; he sees how Leigh Anne has trapped him. That's the first step, learning to see—once you're there, the spell is half-broken.

"Do you have a guitar here?" Betty asks.

"Of course," Thomas says. "You want me to get it out?"

"Please," she says.

He takes out the guitar and strums hesitantly, giving her a sheepish smile.

"It's a cheapo," he says.

He begins to strum and sing, quietly at first, as if he's embarrassed, but then with a clear, strong voice—an old country standard that Betty has heard before, a murder ballad about a man who kills the girl who refused to marry him—a surprisingly sweet-sounding song, considering the subject matter. Betty is so taken with the song that she doesn't notice the door to the back room open. She turns to see a woman standing in the living room doorway.

She can immediately tell that Leigh Anne was once beautiful, maybe shockingly so. She has a round, small face that reminds Betty of Audrey Hepburn, in a way. She is wearing a loose T-shirt, and, to Betty's embarrassment, nothing but underwear. Her legs are also nice-looking but—like the rest of her body—too thin somehow. She looks underfed. As she moves her mouth to speak, Betty notices the cords of muscle in her neck twitching.

"Thomas," she says. "I was sleeping."

"Oh, baby," Thomas says. "I'm so sorry."

"I told you I didn't want you to wake me up."

"Right. I'm sorry. I'll put the guitar away."

"All right," Leigh Anne says.

She turns to Betty, as if she has only just now noticed her.

"Hello," she says.

"Hello," Betty says.

"I'm going back to bed," she says.

Without any more conversation, Leigh Anne turns and heads back into the dark bedroom.

The streetlamp outside the front window winks on. Betty looks down at the remains of her salad, by now wilted, and tries to smile. When she looks back up at Thomas, she can tell that the smile won't do any good. He keeps sneaking glances back into the bedroom, and Betty knows she has lost him.

Although she knows everything is now pointless, she gets up and goes to the window. From here she can see the outline of the Society Hill towers. It isn't really her place, but she opens the window to let the breeze in. It's a fine night outside, she notices.

"You have a lovely view," she says.

"That's true," Thomas says, in the same way he might say *sure*, or *I hear you*.

"Let's have another glass of whiskey," Betty says. She tries to make her voice sound sly.

"Oh," Thomas says, picking up both of their plates. "I should probably clean all this up."

Down on the street, Betty watches Thomas's light go out. On the way home, she regrets saying those last few things in front of the window. What was she trying to accomplish?

Many people warned Betty about Will, but she never believed them. She made every excuse for his behavior; she said it was because his parents neglected him, because he'd been beaten by his uncle as a kid. She said it was because nobody had ever loved him the way she loved him, and he was afraid she would leave him—until one day she did. When you get in a situation like that, nobody can free you but yourself.

THE NEXT SHIFT TOGETHER, neither Betty nor Thomas talk much about their dinner.

"Thanks for coming over," he tells her.

"No problem," she says. "I had a nice time."

But somehow she knows that he will never ask her over for dinner again. Not that he is any less friendly to her at work, but he isn't any friendlier to her, either. He simply treats her the way he treats everybody—perfectly warmly.

At a certain point, months later, Betty begins to see the lie at the heart of Thomas's life. She watches him, one shift, giving the same warm greetings to each customer in turn, as if every one of them were his favorite, as if he waited every day for them to show up so that he could brighten their day. If you're warm to everyone only to a certain point, she reasons, then are you really warm at all?

She begins to see Thomas's warmth as just a certain type of coldness—a reflex—so that no one gets close enough to see what is really going on with him, the strange relationship that keeps him trapped in a house with Leigh Anne. The control Leigh Anne exerts over him begins to strike her as creepy, and she tries to avoid being in the room with him when his phone rings, so as not to hear the quiet, subservient tone he adopts when speaking to her.

She gives up on Thomas; there's no other word for it. One day she gives in to one of Valerie's repeated invitations to go out clubbing with her girlfriends, and while it isn't what she would have chosen for a Saturday night—blue lights and loud music, too much makeup and little conversation—the mass of motion distracts her from being lonely, and when she goes home, the exhaustion she feels from dancing sends her right to sleep. She likes some of the girls, she reasons. She could see them becoming easy friends, just by seeing each other on a regular basis.

It comes as no surprise to anyone, really, when Thomas comes in with a ring two months later.

"We're moving to Massachusetts," he says. "Isn't that hard to believe? There's a meditation center there. Leigh Anne's been doing meditation, and it's really helping."

And later, at the end of the shift, he gets Betty alone in the utility closet. "You seem a little skeptical," he says, like it's a joke. "You must not like New England very much."

Betty has that feeling once again that Thomas feels some special connection with her, too, that the whole thing hasn't been an illusion, concocted in her solitary mind. But what does it matter, now that he's leaving? And where would that connection have led to, even if he'd stayed?

"It's just big news, that's all," she says. "A brand new start. It'll take time to get used to."

"It does seem that way," Thomas says. She wonders how deeply he really listens when people talk to him about the future. "But I won't forget you. I'll write; I'll keep in touch."

His sadness seems authentic, but she has a hard time believing in it. There's no use investing any more emotion in him, now that's decided to bind himself even more tightly to a person who can only make him miserable, and all Betty can muster is a low-level sort of pity. Some people get out, she thinks, and some people don't.

A FEW MONTHS PASS. Betty falls in with some of the girls who are less close with Valerie, sharper and a little more cynical than the rest of her crowd—Betty finds their honesty refreshing. They talk obliquely about their past mistakes: drunk boyfriends in worthless bands, college debt, dead friends they never quite forgave. Betty doesn't tell them everything, but she drops hints of her own, enough for them to recognize that she's been wounded and let her in to the circle of survivors. One day, she thinks, she'll tell them everything.

Another six months and Betty wonders if maybe she might go to graduate school. She writes her undergraduate advisor, who, to her surprise, remembers her well and would be more than happy to write her a recommendation. *So good to hear from you, dear,* she writes. *We were afraid you'd fallen off the face of the earth.*

There's the solace she keeps in the fact that she isn't as wild as some of the people she's become friendly with; she has some money saved up, because she lives more meagerly than the rest of her friends. She keeps the same job—the routine is comforting. She knows that she is the reliable one; she has come to accept it.

Then, one day, a year and a half after his departure, a letter arrives from Thomas.

It starts with a couple of apologies for taking so long

to write and a hope that the letter will find her if she's moved. He explains that things were rough for a while, that after the move they bounced back and forth between various friends' houses before he and Leigh Anne got settled, and that there wasn't much time to write.

But, he goes on, an amazing thing happened—Leigh Anne came into some money when her grandmother died, enough money to put a down payment on a small house near the center where she meditates, and now they have a place to live. He works as the manager of a small permaculture farm, which is something he would like to explain to her if he had the time. The money is better than he expected.

And now, he said, *we have a baby! We named him Lev— you know, like in Tolstoi.* (He spells it, Betty notices, in the Russian manner.)

He ends like this: *I've always been sorry that we didn't become better friends. I felt like you and I always had a lot in common, but we both seemed a little shy, as if we didn't quite know how to start. If you ever have a break from work, I'd like you to come up to Massachusetts and visit. Leigh Anne and Lev and I would all love to have you.*

He includes his phone number—a landline, he notes, because cell phone service is pretty much nonexistent in their small town.

Betty reads the letter a few times. It's now early summer again, and downstairs, below her apartment, she can hear families moving their kids down to the outdoor mall of South Street, arguing with each other. She hasn't been in a relationship since leaving Will. For a while she reasoned that it was trauma, but now it's simply a lack of trust in the whole idea. She doesn't like to admit it, but the idea of relying so strongly on another person has come to seem a little sinister to her, parasitic even.

She would like to imagine Thomas happy, because it would prove some of these conclusions wrong. So, one night when she doesn't have anything else to do, when everyone else is out at some new restaurant, she gives him a call. He is putting the baby to bed. He is glad to hear from her.

Soon they're talking to each other frequently: twice a month, then once a week, sometimes twice. Their first conversations are a bit hesitant, strangely formal; she doesn't know why she's calling, or what she's looking for—but Thomas soon makes things easier. There's a lot to explain; his life is so busy that she can barely imagine it, holding the baby in a sling while he tramps across the fields and grows plants with names that Betty has never heard of, but which Thomas says are so well suited to the environment that he barely has to tend to them: paw paws and Good King Henry, Jerusalem artichokes.

Despite all this, however, Betty begins to feel that Thomas is obscurely dissatisfied. He asks so many questions about the city: about stores he used to visit, bars he remembers fondly. And late one night, just as Betty is about to get off the phone and go to bed—it feels a bit indiscreet to take the phone into her bedroom—Thomas asks her something that takes her aback.

"Would you do me a favor?" he asks. "Would you go to the window and tell me how the skyline looks?"

Betty does as she is told. She describes the blue light, the yellow windows, and when she is done, there's a pause on the other line.

"Just like my old apartment," he says—not *ours*, but *mine*.

"Do you remember when I came over to your house for dinner?" she asks, feeling bold. "What a mess!"

"I didn't think so," he tells her, sounding confused. "But you never did come back."

"No," Betty agrees. "I guess I didn't."

They both pause, and for a moment Betty thinks the two of them are together in her apartment, looking out the window.

"You should come visit," he tells her. "It's been too long."

He goes on for ten minutes, trying to convince her: about the smell of the pine woods through an open car window; the coffee roaster down the street, good as anything in the city; the eerie calls of the owls in the woods. He doesn't realize that Betty has already made up her mind.

SHE TAKES A LONG WEEKEND OFF. The bosses are surprised, even a little happy that she's taking some time; she rarely ever calls in sick or takes a weekend, and when they hear that it's for a trip, they wish her a happy journey. Despite the fact that she has more friends than ever, Betty has come to realize that there are people, including her bosses, who feel that she ought to be having more fun.

It's strange to think that, even though she's barely thirty-two, certain people already consider her an old maid.

She doesn't have a car, and instead of renting one—which seems like too much of a hassle—she decides to take the bus. The Greyhound station is practically empty on a Thursday morning. There are a few people with their families in tow—poor people, Betty imagines, because anybody with any money would have a car or take a plane. But she tells herself that she ought to think more positively, and when she looks with her positive eyes, she notices fathers playing calmly with their children, mothers holding babies with contented expressions in front of the candy machines. The bus comes on time.

On the ride she tries to imagine what changes Thomas might have gone through. Maybe his time in isolation has made him a more open and honest person, now that he doesn't feel the need to be friendly on command. Maybe Leigh Anne is healthier, and he has more freedom to be himself. She imagines him playing his guitar in his new house as the baby sleeps—he could sing lullabies to his son, and old country ballads.

It takes eight hours to Springfield and another hour to Greenfield, but it doesn't seem that long. Betty has always been the sort of person who can retreat into her own head when the situation calls for it, so that small amounts of time can pass by as if they only barely happened.

Thomas meets her at the bus station. He's changed a little—he's thinner than she remembers, and he sports a bushy red beard that softens the lines of his face.

"Where's the baby?" she asks, because she can't think of a proper way to say hello.

Thomas smiles. "I left him at home. You'll get to see him soon enough!"

In the pickup she makes fun of him for going rural, and they talk about the time that's passed.

"You don't look different at all," he says.

"You do," she says. "That beard, the flannel—you look like a mountain man."

"I live in the mountains," he says, laughing. "Those are the Berkshires out your window, you know."

The truck is an old model, and the front cab is all one seat. Their legs are uncomfortably close as they go up the mountain toward the place where Thomas lives. Everything seems to be green and wet, and the dirt everywhere is puddled with mud from a sudden rain. Betty sees stunned people on the side of the road, walking around in their yards as if they've just woken up from a long sleep.

"Rain all the time," Thomas tells her. "It's mud season. Everybody's plans get derailed when their trucks get stuck in the mud."

Betty wonders what would happen if they were stuck in the mud together—the two of them leaning against the hood, considering their options. Would they push the truck up the hill, straining together, or would they wait in the cab until help arrived, happy to be lost for a little while? Despite the winding country roads, and after twenty minutes of driving through pine forests and down Thomas's long dirt driveway, they arrive without any trouble.

AS SOON AS THEY PARK, Thomas takes her on a tour of the property. The house itself is attached to a huge barn, stuck in a clearing surrounded by tall pines. The scale seems much larger than Betty is used to—she feels swallowed up by the landscape. Thomas opens the door of the barn, and Betty sees farming implements, tractors and mowers and sundry tools she can almost guess the purpose of.

"All of my implements," Thomas says, giving her a smirk.

So he's actually become a farmer, Betty thinks. She could never quite believe it, over the phone; it seems like such a solitary occupation for a social person—but then again, someone must help him. She can't imagine him doing everything himself.

On a small hill, visible through the trees, Betty can see a larger white house overlooking the barn.

"That's the Wilcox place," Thomas says. "We bought this house from them. They made a fortune in New York and they thought they'd retire out here, but one of them got sick. They never come out anymore."

"Is it their farm?" Betty asks.

"They own the land," Thomas says. "The business is all mine."

They wander down onto the hill, and Betty can see the rows of vegetables—cabbages and lettuces, purple kale and wide, leafy collards tufting out of the turned earth.

"This is beautiful," she says.

"It's a lot of work," Thomas replies.

He seems almost shy to show her the fields, and the

truth is, she's a little confused. There are only four or five rows here. Not enough to run a business on. In fact, as they walk through the fields, she notices the hills rising on the other side of a small patch of sunflowers and thinks, isn't this really a glorified garden? But she remembers that Thomas had mentioned that Leigh Anne had come into some money. If there's enough of it, then there's no need for him to have a profitable business.

As they walk up the hill, back to the house, everything begins to come together. Thomas is explaining to her how he takes his vegetables to market in two trailers that he and a friend lug behind their bicycles, and Betty realizes: this is Thomas's reward. This is what he got for caring for Leigh Anne for years and years. He stops in the middle of the hill and looks back over the whole expanse, the road tapering down into the carefully cultivated rows of vegetables and then the backdrop of hills topped with cedar and pine.

She guesses she feels happy for Thomas. Certainly she feels, at the top of the hill, her own sense of rootlessness. For more than three years now she has never been able to bear the idea of sacrificing any part of her life to another person, because she never had any idea what she might get in return. Now she knows.

Thomas does something surprising, as they stand there on the hill. He reaches over and takes her hand.

She waits for a minute, looking at the landscape laid out below them. She lets herself imagine that all of it was made for her. Who's to say it wasn't, that Thomas didn't toil in service to Leigh Anne in the hopes that one day Betty would come back, so that he could show it to her, the person he really wanted?

Then she takes her hand back. She doesn't want to look at Thomas, for fear of what might or might not be written on his face. Instead, the two of them walk up to the house in silence.

THE PLACE IS SMALLER THAN she expected. Most of the space in the big structure is taken up by the barn, and the house itself is practically an apartment on stilts. The front is a messy collection of sprouting seedlings in potting soil, greasy cast-iron cookware, and a series of sagging armchairs and couches. Behind the couches she sees a wooden door that must lead back to the bedrooms: the baby's and the one Thomas and Leigh Anne share. It looks to Betty like a bachelor's apartment, except that in one corner a woman is sitting next to a crib. She is looking up from the book she must have recently been reading.

"You're back," the woman says.

Leigh Anne, Betty thinks.

The woman stands up and walks over to them. As she walks, Betty realizes her mistake. The woman can't be Leigh Anne—she's much too young. Her shoulder-length blonde hair is pulled back to show off the fine dusting of freckles on her forehead. She can't be more than twenty-two at the most, Betty thinks. She has the willing enthusiasm of someone not long out of college.

Which is why it is so shocking to her when the woman walks up and kisses Thomas, lightly, almost secretly, on the lips.

"He's sleeping well," she says.

"Thanks for watching him," Thomas says.

"Of course," she whispers, leaning in close.

The woman angles her head toward Betty.

"It's nice to meet you, Betty," she says. "I'm Adrienne. Thomas talks so much about you."

"Right," Betty says.

"I'd better be going home," she says. "*She's* still sleeping."

"Of course," Thomas says.

This time he's the one who kisses her. He lingers longer. And then, with a quick wave in Betty's direction, the woman is gone.

"Who's that?" Betty asks.

"That's Adrienne," Thomas says, as if it's an offhand piece of information. "She comes and helps me out every once in a while."

Betty doesn't know what to say. Instead, she walks over to the crib and looks down at the baby she has waited what seems like a long time to see.

It would be a lie to say that she hadn't imagined what it might look like, whether it would look at all like Leigh Anne, from the little she remembers of her face, or whether it would be a little image of Thomas. It would be a lie to say that she didn't sometimes imagine it looking a little like herself, as if it might be their baby, and not his and Leigh Anne's.

The baby looks like Thomas. She's shocked, in fact, to see how much it looks like him, even at such a young age—she supposes that Thomas always had a boyish face. The baby turns in his sleep, and Betty feels that if he were to open his eyes, he might be staring directly at her. The thought makes her feel guilty.

As she's leaning over the crib, she realizes that it's gotten much darker in the small amount of time that they were touring the farm. It must be like this in the mountains—it takes very little time for the sun to dip over the horizon line and leave the valley in darkness.

OVER THE NEXT FEW HOURS they watch the baby sleep. Thomas talks to her about his life, the difficulty of getting a farm started, the labor he needs but doesn't always get from his friends and associates, but Betty isn't really listening. She realizes, dimly, that she is in some kind of shock, but she also feels it has something to do with the women who keep interrupting their conversations.

The first one is named Ellen. She comes in an hour after Adrienne leaves, knocking lightly on the door. Unlike Adrienne, she seems older than Thomas. She drops off a casserole dish full of black-eyed peas and kale.

"You need to eat better," the woman tells him. The wide plastic bracelets on her wrist jingle.

Thomas holds her in his arms a little, on the other side of the door. Betty wonders if he thinks he's hidden, or if he's doing it brazenly. It's hard to tell.

Then the woman goes, and Thomas comes back. He offers her some of the food. She doesn't want to eat it, but what choice does she have? She's hungry.

"Where were we?" he asks. "Oh right, permaculture crop cycles."

The next visitors are two women, both in their early twenties, both with short hair and the kind of baggy short pants that Betty associates with women who do yoga.

"Will you come to the next group meditation?" they ask, almost in unison.

Thomas assures them that he will. He kisses each of them on the cheek in turn, and then they leave.

Betty begins to panic. Where is Leigh Anne? Why isn't she out here witnessing this? She wonders if she will ever go behind the back door and see the bedrooms. It seems possible that she might go this entire visit without seeing her.

"Would you like to help me take Lev to his room?" Thomas asks.

Betty nods. What else can she do?

Thomas lifts him gently—Betty can't help noticing how smooth and purposeful his arm motions are—and begins to carry him back toward the door. Betty follows behind, and although the prospect of opening the door frightens her, she steels, herself and passes through in Thomas's wake.

Behind the door are two small rooms set off by naked drywall and simple wooden doors. They pass through the left door and into the baby's room—a small recessed bed with a wooden mobile hanging over it, the little pieces of wood hanging over the blankets carved into the shape of dolphins.

The baby barely makes a sound. He fidgets a little and then falls directly back to sleep.

"He's so easy," Thomas says, leaning against the room's bare frame. "Sometimes I can't believe how lucky I am."

The spot where he is leaning is very close to her. The one window in the room looks out over the Wilcox's place, vacant and desolate on the top of the hill. Betty remembers the time many years ago when she stood in front of the windows of his apartment and hoped that he would come and stand next to her to watch lights in other people's houses. Now she has the distinct feeling that he is closing the gap between the two of them. She can sense him moving along the wall.

A voice comes through the thin walls—quiet, but also harsh, as if the vocal cords making it are dried out.

"Thomas," it says. "Are you there?"

Thomas sighs, so softly Betty wouldn't have noticed it if he weren't so close that she could almost feel his breath on her cheek.

"One minute," he says.

He creeps out of the baby's room. Pressed up against the wall, Betty can hear the conversation clearly.

"Are you in there with someone?" the voice asks.

"It's just my friend, Betty," he says.

There is a long pause. Betty thinks she can hear labored breathing.

"I'm thirsty," the voice says. "Can you get me some water?"

"Of course," Thomas says. "I'm just putting Lev to bed."

"Is he asleep?" the voice asks, suddenly plaintive. "Is he asleep?"

"Yes," Thomas says. "He's asleep."

Betty can't take it anymore. She moves out toward the edge of the doorway, quietly enough that she thinks no one will notice. She leans out and looks through the door into Leigh Anne and Thomas's bedroom.

She isn't sure what she expected to find, but the scene is darker than she imagined: there's only a small reading light clamped to the headboard of a huge four-poster that takes up almost the entire room. There are two tables, both of which are littered with bottles and eyedroppers, mason jars full of different liquids—tinctures, Betty assumes—and a small antique alarm clock, stopped at midnight.

Thomas is picking up a few of the mason jars, tidying up. Leigh Anne is lying in the middle of the bed, wearing a nightgown. Betty can't make her out that well—she's blurry in the low light. Slowly, with obvious effort, Leigh Anne tries to lift herself into a sitting position.

"Relax," Thomas says, his voice soothing. "I'll get you that water."

Leigh Anne falls back.

"Is something the matter?" she asks. "I feel like something's wrong."

"Of course not," Thomas says. "We just finished up dinner."

"I had a bad dream," Leigh Anne says, in a worried voice that reminds Betty of a child's.

Thomas brushes the reading lamp with his back, and the sudden movement of the light exposes Leigh Anne's arm—so shockingly thin that Betty can almost see the two bones traveling downward to her wrist. Leigh Anne shrinks away from the light and puts her arm under the blanket.

"I'll get you some water," Thomas says.

Leigh Anne nestles into the bed, looking for sleep.

Betty hears him coming for the door, and she moves back behind the wall. She realizes that she is hiding. She looks over at the Wilcox place, which is dark. Then her eye falls on the baby, still asleep, unaware of what's going on.

PERHAPS THE MOST DISTURBING of all the cases Betty read about in the years when she was in love with Thomas—she resists admitting it, even now, but she knows it's true; she was in love with the idea of him, of how he might be the light that led her back to the world—was the story of Josef Fritzl, the Austrian man who locked his daughter in a basement.

Josef Fritzl had been abusive to his daughter, Elisabeth, from the time she was eleven years old. When it became clear that the girl was going to run away from home—she attempted an escape once, when she was eighteen, but was brought home by the police—he began to convert his basement into a prison cell. When his daughter began preparing to leave home for a waitressing job in the nearby city of Linz, Fritzl lured her into the basement, drugged her with ether, and then locked her inside.

Over the next twenty-four years, Josef Fritzl repeatedly raped his daughter, who gave birth to seven children.

Three of the children were raised by Fritzl and his wife Rosemarie; the others either died of childhood illnesses or remained locked in the basement with their mother.

Despite the obvious horrific details—the low ceilings in the prison that caused the boy children to become hunchbacks, Fritzl's threats that the doors were electrically charged and that Valerie and her children would be gassed if they tried to escape, the denial of food and water if they "misbehaved"—what frightened Betty most about the story (for she was trying to frighten herself in those days, to remind herself why she needed to be alone) was the fact that no one seemed to notice that anything was wrong. Fritzl's wife, Rosemarie, for example, always maintained that she had never known anything about the situation in the cellar—the torture, rape, and smaller cruelties that went on every day below her feet. She knew her husband went down every morning at nine o'clock to work on plans for machines that he sold to various engineering firms. He was not to be disturbed during his work. That, she said, was the extent of her knowledge and thus the proof of her innocence—their relationship simply didn't permit her to go down to the basement.

Now, as she stands in the front room of Thomas's house, Betty looks out the front window into a stand of trees. She sees lights dancing out there; she thinks they must be fires, or dancing flashlights.

"What are those lights?" Betty asks.

Thomas is behind her. He is looking out at the forest too, and Betty can sense that fairly soon he will encircle her waist with his arms.

"Those are the girls," Thomas says. "They come up every summer to help me with the farm. It's a worker program, I guess. They're out there every night, whooping it up. Sometimes they come for dinner."

Betty tries to think of a question that might make sense to ask. She thinks: do they know who lives in your bedroom? She thinks: where do you have sex with them, outside or right here in the living room with the baby in its crib? She thinks: is there someone I can tell about this who might do something?

"You could stay here for a while," he tells her, his mouth close to her ear. "If you wanted. Lord knows I could use the help."

These are the words she's always waited for: on the phone, in the truck on the way to the farm, even as they climbed the steps to this ghastly apartment on stilts, before she knew about Leigh Anne sleeping in the back room. Now, as she watches the girls in the forest dancing in front of the firelight, she tries to find a strategy to refuse. She will let Thomas put his arms around her waist. She will spend the night on the couch, complaining of a stomachache. Then, the next morning, she will tell Thomas she has an emergency at home, and he will drive her to the bus station.

She would like another strategy, something that would change the situation, not just for Leigh Anne, but for all those women: the bank tellers, their heads encircled by rope; the poets beaten in closets; the wives who claim they have seen and heard nothing out of the ordinary. But who would she talk to, to put things right? The girls in the forest don't seem to care, and she doubts very much that this is a matter for the police. Maybe she'll tell her girlfriends, after she escapes; they'll be horrified, sure, but helpless to do anything other than mark off another man not to be trusted, another dream to avoid believing.

Too late now to talk to Leigh Anne, to take her by the shoulders and shake her thin body. What would Betty say, except, *I was where you are now, once before, and for a long time I wanted to take your place*?

The baby begins to cry, and Leigh Anne moans. Thomas slips away, apologizing. "One minute," he says, slipping through the door. He quiets Leigh Anne, he sings the baby a song:

> *Buffalo gals won't you come out tonight*
> *come out tonight, come out tonight*
> *Buffalo gals won't you come out tonight*
> *and dance by the light of the moon.*

Everything here is consensual: a matter between husband and a wife, unquestionable. The only person Betty can save is herself. She will play along with the conspiracy of silence and pretend that nothing is wrong. She will use this strategy, the one that works, and it will work again.

LOVE GOES TO
A BUILDING ON FIRE
\\\\\\\\

MEETING YOU, RAMONA, made me realize that all the buildings in our city are in love. Probably it was always this way, but before I didn't notice. Sometimes the love is subtle, as with an office building in winter; only the lighting system flickers. In other seasons, in other buildings, the love is more obvious: hair salons, bingo parlors, gymnasiums in spring. These buildings throb at the edges, warm to the touch.

There is office love, stalking the marble hallways of the skyscrapers. It dangles on sharp edges, pining for a comfortable chair. Do you remember the way we met, in the middle of the yellow hall, the silence and the typewriters chattering like teeth? We got out of that building as quick as we could, because office romance never lasts.

There is satisfied love, lingering in the brownstones, glowing with money. On the abandoned nights of early February, when the other buildings huddled in the cold, you and I walked past the palatial estates near Rittenhouse Square and watched love settle in their porthole windows like melted butter.

"That's the kind of place I'd like to live in when I'm old," I told you.

But you said it seemed a little stodgy, and now I see what you mean—the fat lights, the lazy dogs, the way love sinks under the weight of all that brick until only the basement trembles.

I USED TO COMPLAIN THAT you changed your mind too quickly, Ramona, but now I see it was a matter of physical laws; you can't fight the way the pressure in a room changes any more than I can fight the pull of gravity.

"You're too finicky," I said. "The trick is to pick something and stick there."

But you couldn't stick anywhere; you flew through the door like the noblest of gasses.

We were always on the move. We started in a basement apartment because that was all we could afford, and isn't it best to be in the dark when you're starting out? Love grows best in the darkness, in the company of certain subterranean sounds—heartbeats, whispering, and the constant possibility of a train.

You said the air there was stale, so we moved above-ground. We got ourselves a little room in a collective house where the windows were fogged with the steam from lentil soup and the air was full of compressed sex. You decorated our blue walls with gramophone needles and balls of twine. I alphabetized the record collection.

But the air was too thick, you said—stuffed to bursting with the clatter of drums and the stiff syllables of political conversations—you could barely breathe, you had to get out of there. So in a time of great danger, in which our love was as vulnerable to the elements as a hermit crab without a shell, we moved into an apartment—one giant room, actually: a bedroom that met a living room that met a kitchen. The autumn dropped, and the baseboard heating made the walls bloom despite the cold.

If love keeps growing, it requires a house. That's how I felt, anyway. It was the fall, our credit was good, and the market was there for the taking.

"Think about the future," I said. "If we're going to make a life for ourselves, we need room to expand."

But you were worried about the sheer size of a house and its responsibilities. Back then you knew things that I am still in the process of learning. You knew that every neighborhood in this city contains at least one house that was too big to fill. The result is a vacuum, which swallows the residents, their neighbors, and sometimes the entire block.

These days I go walking and I see a long series of shuttered windows, empty of love, inviting to arsonists.

I tried to tell you that a satisfied house is as close as our city gets to a chapel—its eyes are open and its windows are full of glowing fruit. But you always pointed out the difficulty in building one.

THE FALL WORE AWAY TO WINTER, and the wind came like a cupped hand against my back. Still we went around the city, arguing about what exactly defined a building. The subway, for instance—that one was clear. A subway is just a series of tubes, too big to be filled with love. Its walls are cold, its businesses are bound to fail, and its people are sallow and perpetually unsatisfied.

One time you and I got lost in those tunnels, trying to figure out how to transfer to New Jersey. I remember you said it was lonely, and you shivered, imagining what it would be like to live down there with the rats and exhausted commuters.

Do you remember the terrible argument we had that November about whether a church is a building? I said it resembles one on Fridays, Sundays, and alternate Wednesdays. But what about the other days, you pointed out? On other days it resembles one of those hollowed ruins the city marks for demolition.

Sometimes I think the question of a church is whether someone can be in love only most of the time.

IN WINTER, RAMONA, the buildings on our block began to shrink. Stray cats skittered through the expanding alleyways. Some people were lucky and found a space inside, while other people were left exposed to the elements. You and I stood in the window, holding onto each other, and looked out at the unlucky people stranded in the cold.

But our love, pressurized by decreasing space, glowed more fiercely in the glass. I'm sure you remember that increase in pressure, Ramona—the weight in our hands, in our throats. We hardly went outside anymore, because of the weather, and sometimes just a little motion was enough to set off small explosions inside our paper-thin walls.

You said you felt like I was watching you all the time, that you couldn't get away from me, that there were no other rooms to escape to. Who else was I supposed to look at, Ramona? Our love had gotten so big that there was nothing else to see. You paced around the apartment, pulling down curtains and picture frames, throwing records out of their order and scattering them across the floor, but even while you raged, the love was still growing, pressing at the edges of the walls.

Still we were afraid of the outside. We saw what the thin atmosphere did to the people who were caught in the winter air. The cold drew the heat from their bodies, the light of the street lamps was dim, and words seemed to disappear the minute they were spoken. Everyone seemed to be wandering, distant and lonely.

It is difficult to survive for very long in the winter without a building, Ramona. I remember the day I picked up my bags and moved out into the street, watching you in the window as you waved. I always thought you would be the one to go, the one who had the least faith in the idea of buildings in the first place, and I felt bitter, standing there in the cold air with one chapped hand wrapped around the handle of a faded red duffel bag and the other one pleading with the air.

SOME PEOPLE SAY A BUILDING doesn't need love to survive. Look at the Federal Building, they say, with its metal detectors and persistent smell of singed plastic. There's no love behind the well-armed security guards.

I say that the people who go into the Federal Building—the passionate prosecutors in their high heels, the protestors with their overwhelming attachment to injustice—bring their love with them. A building with that much traffic never wants for love; it's the houses we have to worry about.

Ever since I left you, Ramona, I've had a habit of walking by the house where we used to live. It sits in a block that was hit hard by the mortgage crisis. Half of the places are shuttered, their windows boarded over, like eyes that have been closed by morticians.

But hope springs eternal. No matter the police presence, the boards and the metal bars, an empty building is an invitation to love, and the house where you and I once lived is definitely occupied—I see shadows moving behind the empty frames. I don't know who lives there, although I have my theories. Addict love, so singular as to be frightening. Squatter love, which is doomed. That kind of love lingers, long after the men in the hazmat suits have cleared the other detritus away.

This year, in the wake of some government failure, angry residents set whole blocks of the southwestern part of the city on fire. Citizens in other neighborhoods cowered indoors, afraid to go outside. Even I wondered: *Will this be what happens when the love in my life dies? Will my neighbors set me on fire and spread my ashes on the thin grass?*

It comforts me a little to walk the city, Ramona, thinking about you. I don't know where you are now, whether you're happy or unhappy, if you've found a place to live that suits you—but your way of seeing is still with me. Maybe you were more tender than I imagined. Maybe it was your love filling all these buildings, maybe all these theories are only your theories that I've learned by heart and told other people as if they were my own. But at least I don't have to worry about my own love burning down. When fire comes to a building, Ramona, you have long since disappeared.

HUSBANDRY
\\\\\\\\\

ONE SATURDAY MORNING, three months after her father's death, Cheryl wakes up early—barely gray dawn—to find her mother sitting at the kitchen table, a rifle in her hands.

The kitchen is arrayed for breakfast. The coffeepot drips. Bacon fat congeals in the cast-iron pan. Above the burners, on the part of the wall behind the stove's dirty hood, a sign in needlepoint reads: Martha Stewart Doesn't Live Here.

Her mother does not drink coffee or enjoy bacon. These were her father's favorites.

Cheryl likes bacon. She's not so sure about coffee, a privilege she's never been allowed.

"Go ahead," her mother says. "Help yourself."

Her mother's appearance is confusing. No makeup, but traces of it from yesterday, shadows of vanished eyeliner that clash with the rest of her outfit: her father's favorite fall hunting jacket, a soft mass of quilted fabric in a camouflage pattern.

Cheryl stands in the doorway, unsure of how to proceed. "Where are you going?"

Her mother strokes the rifle's barrel with a sad expression, as if the gun were a sick animal she was taking to the hospital, or else out back, to put it out of its misery. "Henry said he'd take me along today."

Henry is one of her father's friends—if you can call men "friends" who only see each other on Saturdays in autumn, talking little, driving out on cold mornings to shoot deer.

"Hunting?" Cheryl asks.

Her mother nods softly. She is a tall woman, taller than Cheryl's father had been, and the hunting jacket doesn't look as ridiculous on her as it might have on someone smaller. Still, she seems uncomfortable swaddled in its folds.

Her mother has never hunted before—not to Cheryl's knowledge. She wonders if the gentle way her mother strokes the barrel is an attempt to learn the rifle's use by touch alone.

A horn calls from outside, Henry's two soft bleats. Cheryl knows the sound by heart. It sometimes breaks her hazy Saturday sleep, entering her dreams.

Her mother gets up. "Have coffee if you want." The kitchen light shows remnants of powder in the lines of her face. She has a hard time holding the gun and opening the door at the same time.

Once her mother is gone, Cheryl takes her coffee out onto the porch, overlooking the north end of Boyer Street. She strains her eyes toward the center of town, across from the Crosby General Store, where the gingko berries fall around the historic monument: orange-yellow ovals, un-crushed by human feet. The light is up; a mourning dove coos. Cheryl's favorite bird, with its throaty cry. It makes its own echo.

Cheryl wants to become an ornithologist. She's good at biology.

The coffee is bitter, but she drinks it all.

CHERYL HAS NEVER BEEN HUNTING—except for once, when she was seven and her mother was away at a con-ference in Middletown. Cheryl only remembers snatches: the shadows of men moving quietly between trees, a rifle blast shattering the air. They say the deer carcass—drip-ping blood, two men carrying it between them—made her sick, but Cheryl doesn't remember. Whenever her father and Henry joked about it, she would wonder if they made it up to remind her she was a girl.

Not that she ever wanted to repeat the experience; not that hunting seemed *fun*. On Saturdays Cheryl sometimes found her father at the table, hands wrapped around a cof-fee cup, complaining. His joints ached, his back ached, he'd rather stay in the hammock out back, drinking beer and reading car magazines.

On days when he came back with a deer, Cheryl would

watch him through the window of the garage, hanging the field-dressed carcass on a hook, cutting the hide from lip to breastbone, removing the skin of the face to expose the naked teeth. He put on talk radio and went about his work in slow silence, the way she imagined people worked in factories—as her father had, once, as a teenager, before getting his job as a salesman.

IT DOESN'T TAKE LONG for word to get out about her mother's hunting trip. Cheryl assumes Henry's wife Edna is to blame; everyone knows Edna is a gossip. They must have had a telephone chain that Saturday, spreading the news, because by the time Cheryl sits down in the high school cafeteria on Monday, all the girls from Danville— all her friends in the world—think they know the story.

"Your mom bring anything back?" Marcie asks, as if it were a casual question.

"Nah, bet she didn't," Jennifer says. "Prolly ain't much of a shot."

Cheryl wishes she could be at one of the other tables, with kids from Mullica Corners, or Watertown, or Stow Creek, any of the other tribes where cruel talk is kept less brazen, out of respect for grief.

"Well, I think it shows respect," Molly says.

Molly is Cheryl's best friend, but today everything about her seems silly: her blue track suit with a horse logo emblazoned on the chest, the yellow bands that keep her hair up in double tails.

"You know," Molly adds. "Respect for your dad."

"Shut up, Molly," Cheryl says, low and hard, so everyone will know she's serious.

Molly looks down at the hands folded in her lap. Cheryl can hear the boys at the next table, discussing the Sixers' chances for a championship.

"It's not right," Tristan says. "Your mom shouldn't try to take on your dad's role. Men and women are made different in God's image."

Tristan is the only boy at their table and the official tenth-grade amateur theologian. The girls tolerate him, Cheryl thinks, because they assume he's gay, though whether he knows that himself is unclear. Usually Cheryl sympathizes with his confusion, but today he seems small and contemptible.

"Fuck God," Cheryl says and gets up to leave.

"Your dad wouldn't have wanted you to say that!" Tristan yells.

TRISTAN IS RIGHT. Cheryl's father—while no churchgoer—would never have wanted her to say something so vicious. Her father was steadfast, decent; when people spoke of him, it was as if they were speaking of a soldier who had died in battle—and this was when he was alive.

Your father, they'd say, *has never said an unkind word in his life.*

This always seemed odd to Cheryl; not because her father wasn't as decent as people thought he was (though sometimes she wondered), but because he had the least decent of human occupations: used-car salesman. Maybe they spoke of him this way because his boss, Ed Presley, was such a terrible person. *Shyster*, people called him—although Cheryl assumed most businessmen had to be shysters, sometimes.

His profession might be dishonest, his products often defective, but Cheryl's father had a way of convincing the customer that although this '92 Impala might have some loose gaskets, it was the best they could hope for in their price range, and if there were any problems, he could recommend a mechanic that would take care of it for much cheaper than the one over at Mullica Corners. But until the process was complete—until the money changed hands, happiness assured—Cheryl's father worried. He was the conduit through which everything flowed.

Cheryl wonders now, after the accident, if her father was ever actually a decent man or if he was simply tormented into it, bullied by forces he couldn't control. He seemed to be always defending himself against some accusation, just around the corner. Can a person live righteously if only out of fear?

NOW HER MOTHER LIVES FEARFULLY, shouldering her father's responsibilities.

Not that Cheryl can blame her for feeling overwhelmed. She works full-time as a guidance counselor at Watertown High, rushes home every afternoon to make dinner, and then, in the little bit of autumn daylight left, she takes tin cans out to the edge of the field and sets them up on the half-broken slats of the wood fence.

Cheryl hears the shots ring out, but they don't hit. Her aim is still poor.

Slowly, though, this changes. In early evening, sitting on the toilet in the back bathroom, Cheryl notices the hollow knock, strangely wooden, of the pierced cans falling.

Her mother has begun drinking coffee. Maybe this helps.

But it isn't her mother's external changes that bother Cheryl: jeans instead of skirts, the silent hours she spends in the garage, once her rifle skills have improved, trying to dress her first kill using an instructional manual.

She doesn't even mind when her mother comes out afterward soaked in blood. At least now she knows the story about her one hunting trip was a lie; she doesn't faint or vomit, watching the stray flies circling her mother's head.

What bothers Cheryl is her mother's inner transformation.

Her father always relied on her mother for lightness. Worn down, worried, he needed her jokes and soothing words. She poured pancakes in the shapes of bears and squirrels. She smelled like lemon and sang songs that were cheesy but full of peace: *And all through my coffee break time—I say a little prayer for you!*

Now her mother mumbles instead of singing, and she stoops. This woman who always carried herself so well, as if she'd walked around balancing books on her head as a child.

Cheryl is embarrassed. People whisper that her mother is *letting herself go*; there are knots in her formerly perfect dirty blonde hair, and she wears the hunting jacket when she runs to check the mail. Who could blame Cheryl for being a little ashamed? No sixteen-year-old girl wants to be the object of public scrutiny, even by relation.

And there are extra duties for Cheryl, now that it's just the two of them—duties she finds unpleasant.

"Why don't you take over some of the cooking?" Her mother's voice is quiet and sad, her dad's old way of speaking. "Just a little help."

So Cheryl doesn't go back to her job at the counter of Stow Creek Sub and Pizza, as she'd planned to, once the mourning period was over; instead she learns the basic tricks of home cuisine: how to smash a clove of garlic with the side of a knife, how to keep rice from burning, how tomatoes give up their juice.

Now Molly comes by in the afternoon, wearing her pink sweatshirt, and finds Cheryl in the kitchen, cooking, her hair up in a messy bun.

"Boys are playing football in the lot," Molly says, tugging her ponytail nervously. "You wanna come out?"

"Busy," Cheryl sighs.

"Fine," Molly says, annoyed. "Suit yourself."

It makes Cheryl feel so *old*.

Maybe if her mother wasn't so silent, Cheryl might not mind acting like a wife. She would have married her old mother in a second and helped her through her troubles, but she doesn't want to be forced into connection with someone so joyless and dutiful, conducting rifle practice in the dim October evening.

Sometimes, when Cheryl is feeling particularly morbid, she imagines her father's ghost is haunting them. Not *them*, really, but her mother's body—making it move and speak in strange new ways.

PERHAPS IF CHERYL'S FATHER hadn't died in such a frightening way, evoked such sympathy from the town, people wouldn't have coddled her mother. Maybe Henry would never have taken her hunting. But given her father's fate, nothing her mother does seems odd.

It happened in the middle of summer, when two men came to the dealership to sell a half-destroyed Dodge Charger. Cheryl wonders sometimes if her father could have treated them differently, given them less hope. He must have known they were tweakers, these towheaded men with buzz cuts, loose white shirts, and darting eyes— what people in Danville called Pineys, living in clearings in the barrens where cops don't go.

He could have turned them away with a convenient excuse, but he told them to come back tomorrow. He would have a talk with his boss.

The towheaded men were excited. They said they'd come back tomorrow for the money.

Cheryl's father only laughed. He said he'd do his best.

Ed Presley, however, was not sympathetic. *Those boys aren't worth your time. Next time you see them, you run them out of here, sweet as you can.*

That night Cheryl's father stayed up late, worrying: had he deceived these men? Even if they were drug-addled, he needed to do right. He had a cousin in Watertown who'd buy the parts, at least. He'd tell them that.

This reassurance let him sleep a little.

The next day the towheaded men pulled up in the lot, their Charger making a high-pitched screeching, probably the timing belt. The men got out, shifting their agitated necks like chickens.

Looks like we won't be able to make a deal, Cheryl's father said. *But a cousin of mine could give you good money for parts.*

One of the towheaded men screamed at him, grabbing his collar. *You led me on, you faggot!*

The other pulled him off, but not before he'd ripped two buttons off Cheryl's father's shirt.

Ed Presley came out from the office, ample belly flopping, sweat beading in the high September sun. *Get outta here, you fucking wasters!*

The towheaded men ran for the car and lit out, burning the road.

Presley was red-faced, holding his knees and panting hard. *I said be* sweet, *Alex—I didn't say fight them!*

Cheryl's father stood there, trembling.

Don't worry. Presley caught his breath. *They're just animals. Worse than animals. Goddamn!*

Her father spent the rest of the day inside the office, doing paperwork. The main façade of the office had floor-to-ceiling glass windows, open to the road, which Presley had always told Cheryl's father *promoted a feeling of transparency in the customer.* So that day, when he was working in the office, Cheryl's father was exposed.

They came up fast, in the gray evening light just before closing, faster than a Charger should have been able to go. Behind the Charger came a mud-splattered F-150, rear bed cluttered with broken machinery. The people in the lot cleared out on either side of them, alerted by the sound of the whining engine and the weird whoops the tweakers gave from behind their broken windows. People dove to either side as the cars went straight for the front office glass, where Cheryl's father sat.

Later Presley sat cross-legged, plucking at grass, oblivious to the cameras.

Animals! He muttered, through tears.

Cheryl saw it on the television screen at Stow Creek Sub and Pizza, where she was working an after-school shift: smoke leaking out of the glass front of the lot office, a ticker tape beneath explaining that the men in the cars were in critical condition, but no mention of her father—not until later.

Now, looking back, she remembers one man in particular who stood beside her in the restaurant, watching the screen—an old man with sagging jowls, holding his MIA veterans' hat over his heart.

ONE SATURDAY EVENING IN MID-OCTOBER, Cheryl is trying to catch up on biology homework while cooking a pot of venison stew, when she smells the telltale signs of burning. She rushes over to the stove and stirs, bringing up black specks, a whole pot ruined.

For thirty minutes she paces the kitchen, close to panic—what will they eat for dinner?—before she hears her mother shuffling through the front door.

Cheryl's anger explodes. "Why do you torture yourself like this?"

Her mother sits down at the kitchen table. Her hunting gear seems less strange—maybe because Cheryl has gotten used to it, maybe because the makeup is long since gone from her face and her eyes are heavy from insomnia, her father's curse.

"I used to think like you," she says eventually. "I used to tell him *stay home*, *kick back*, that the boys could get along without him one time, if he liked. I used to make fun of him sometimes, being so damn dour. *It's my duty*, he said. *Otherwise those deer will ruin everything.*"

Her mother stares at the wall. Her vision plays across it, and for a moment Cheryl thinks her father is standing in the room with them, judging them.

"I asked him, was he really afraid of *deer*? He just shook his head. *We're their only predators, Bobbie Jean. We got to do what's right.*"

Now she turns from the wall and looks Cheryl full in the face, her father's voice coming through her mouth. "I never thought it was real, really—just an excuse to go out with the boys. But then, after what happened, with the cars . . . "

Why can't she say it? Cheryl wonders. She can't name it, so it turns into something else in her mind.

"I was out in the backyard," her mother continues. "It was getting dark, and there were two deer out in the field, cozied up by the fence. I looked, stared 'em down. You ever look at an animal? I mean, really look? You ever try to consider what an animal's *thinking*? I mean, I tried my best, baby girl. I stared for a long time, okay—those damn dark eyes. There's nothing inside. They don't think. It's just *muscle*."

She looks so tired, Cheryl thinks, *but her hands are shaking.*

Her mother pats the stock of the gun.

"So I picked up the gun, baby girl," her mother says, her smile a half grimace. "It *is* a duty."

"There's no dinner," Cheryl says. "I burned it all."

"They'd come in the house, if we let 'em," her mother continues. "Eat up everything we own, sleep in our beds like dogs."

The doorbell rings. Cheryl looks up and sees Edna, Henry's wife, waving through the screen. What a thin, fussy woman—too much foundation, avocado eyeliner.

"I just thought I'd come by and see if you two needed any help," Edna says, voice full of concern, but Cheryl can already see her easing the door open, craning her neck to collect evidence.

"We've got it all under control." Cheryl stands in the doorway of the kitchen, brandishing her ladle. She strides toward the door, fending off the intruder: her right, as woman of the house. She succeeds—Edna backs off without a fight. For now.

"I never liked that woman," Cheryl's mother says afterward.

Cheryl notices the barrel of the gun beneath the table, pointed toward the door. A coincidence.

MAYBE THERE'S ANOTHER REASON that the town, and Henry in particular, lets Cheryl's mother get away with retreating from the world, as if she were some militiaman practicing her shot.

On the day of the funeral, wearing a black dress which was too big for her—her mother always overshot the mark, having been a large girl herself—Cheryl stood in the chapel off of Route 14, trying to fend off well-wishers with her eyes, when she saw an odd episode over by the food table, cluttered with store-bought pies and strange arrangements of cookies and frosting. *Why do people bring sweets to a funeral?*

Standing next to the table, Henry put a hand on her mother's shoulder, and her mother—in shock, of course, and probably only half-conscious of who was standing behind her—put her own hand on top of it.

She didn't know Cheryl was watching. Otherwise she would have never have interlaced her fingers with his.

Cheryl wonders now—a full season after the fact—what Henry was really asking when he offered to take her mother hunting. Was he as surprised as she was, that late September morning, when she came out of the house, dressed to kill, a gun in her unsteady hands?

CHERYL TELLS HERSELF it's only a phase: part of the mourning process. As long as her mother keeps it out of the house, Cheryl thinks. Deer season will soon be over, at least officially—though who knows what private lands Henry might be willing take her to, if she insisted.

Now that Cheryl is the one doing all the cooking, her mother can expand her shooting time. She's free to sit on the back porch, gun at the ready.

As October gives way to November she begins to take shots at small, scurrying creatures. Her eye grows sharper. She can hit a groundhog easy and even a chipmunk at a fair distance, its chubby body barely bigger than a cartridge.

They live far down Boyer, almost at the dead end of the river; if people heard shots, they wouldn't know them from hunter's rifles. Still, Cheryl is afraid Molly will come by one afternoon and find her mother taking potshots. Not that Molly comes by much—Cheryl is too busy to idle away time. The other girls complain she's grown surly.

Cheryl isn't worried for the rodents. When she was in the Brownies, there were girls who went gooey over chipmunks, but Cheryl has always thought of them as rats with fatter faces. It's the birds she can't forgive, the occasional blue jay clipped out of the sky. It's cruel. What harm do birds do?

Then one night she wakes up to the sound of a shot. *That came from inside the house*, she thinks and, rushing downstairs, finds her mother in the living room, gun still hot across her knees, a hole in the screen of the living room window. It's a warm night for October; she has the glass pushed up. A dead mourning dove nestles against the mesh.

"Trying to fly in," her mother explains.

"It wasn't trying to come inside," Cheryl says. "Just sitting in the window!"

"So *you* say." Her mother narrows her eyes.

The limp body bleeds onto the sill. Mourning doves were always her favorite. How could anyone kill a thing that cries so softly?

There is no one for Cheryl to tell, no one she can trust. Both sets of grandparents are dead; her mother was an only child, and her father's cousins live far north of Middletown. She's sure Edna would love to hear—to gossip about her mother's odd habits—but Cheryl has her pride. She won't be the subject of ridicule.

Cheryl has nightmares where her mother's in a field, knocking helpless creatures out of flight. No one in Danville respects the season for common birds. Her mother can shoot them all year round.

CHERYL BEGINS DEVISING A PLAN. One afternoon in early November, Cheryl tells Mr. Bumthwaite, her biology teacher, about a possible science fair project. She needs to know the best way to catch a bird, to tag it, and measure the movement of their local avian population: who flies away for winter, who returns.

Mr. Bumthwaite is happy to oblige, though he worries that the project might be a bit too loose. The two of them look online together. Cheryl takes copious notes, while her teacher looks on approvingly. There are not many children so intent on their studies, and Mr. Bumthwaite likes her, the poor man, oblivious to the taunts of the students, mocking his frizzy hair, his red, swollen fingers, and his eczema. He's been sweeter to her since the accident, and

Cheryl wonders what private tragedy has made him so sympathetic.

On Sunday, while her mother is hunting, Cheryl walks the length of Boyer, carrying a blue milk crate. Cars pass on the way to Danville Presbyterian, children's faces pressed against the glass. Cheryl doesn't care, happy enough to escape her house that she's no longer afraid of meeting Molly on the street.

The milk crate trap is not as easy as it seemed on the Internet. The prop is difficult: it has to be firm enough to keep the crate upright, but light enough to fall at the slightest touch. It takes the entire afternoon to trap a tiny sparrow. It flutters against the milk crate's walls, almost small enough to slip through the handle.

It takes great restraint to avoid tipping back the plastic and letting it free, but in the end Cheryl does as planned: drapes a sheet over the crate and slides the excess underneath, using an elastic band to keep the bird inside.

She puts the bird in a cage in her room, placing a sheet over it to keep it quiet when her mother comes home. She worries about feeding—a little sparrow needs to eat so much, or else it dies.

A few days later—by which time Cheryl has another sparrow, a finch, and a thin-legged bird with a tufted head she cannot seem to identify—she is leaving her room when her mother appears at the top of the stairs.

"Are there birds in the house?" she asks. "I keep hearing noises."

"What I do in my room is my business," Cheryl says.

She opens the door, reaches for the opposite handle, and turns the interior lock.

When she comes home, later that evening, she sneaks around the roof of their wraparound porch and shimmies into her room through an unlocked window. At the last moment she slips and falls flat on her bedroom floor.

The tittering birdsong is like laugher, but Cheryl doesn't mind, even if it's at her expense. How long has it been since anyone laughed in this house? She feels a tinge of conscience, to think she has to silence them.

WE'RE GONNA HAVE a hell of a Thanksgiving this year.

Cheryl's mother repeats this like a mantra. Sometimes it seems she's convincing herself, psyching herself up for some kind of accomplishment, as if she must kill enough deer to provide a full table for all of their relatives—although Cheryl's fairly certain no dinner has been planned and no relatives invited.

Sometimes it seems as if her mother is stating a clear and difficult fact, the way an old man might speak after the first snowfall of the season: *It's gonna be a hell of a winter this year.*

And other times—as on Sunday morning, three weeks into November, her mother sitting in the kitchen in what looks to Cheryl like despair, staring at the far wall as if it were a glass window and some kind of tragedy were playing out behind it—she says it as if she is fully aware of how absurd the situation has become, as she might have back when she was a carefree kind of mother, burning a roast and saying, *It's gonna be a hell of a dinner tonight.*

Only her voice is much drier and deader than it was, those many months ago; low and harsh, even threatening, the way a boy might say to another boy in the school parking lot, smacking fist to palm: *We're gonna have a hell of a time, you and me.*

"I've let you down, baby girl," her mother says. "I didn't mean to."

"What do you mean, Mom?" Cheryl asks.

"It's gonna be a hell of a Thanksgiving," her mother says. She puts her forehead in her arms and cries.

For the first time, Cheryl feels frightened. A teenage girl is a kind of animal too, and lately her mother doesn't seem to see her, staring as if she can't quite place her presence—and when she does focus, she seems suspicious, like she senses Cheryl has a plan.

Her mother gets up slowly, tapping the rifle stock against her palm, and heads out to the back door to get ready for hunting.

She is still out back when Henry's horn comes from across the grass.

Cheryl gets up from her seat and rushes out the door. Henry is in his truck, mud splattered on the pitted hood. She goes toward him, arms raised, as if she were flagging him down to help in an accident.

"What's the matter, Cher?" Henry asks.

Cher is her father's nickname. The two men are quite alike: black T-shirts with pockets in front to hold their cigarettes, the smell of nicotine and sweat. Cheryl has to resist the powerful urge to lay her head on his shoulder and cry.

It comes out in a rush: how her mother has turned sour and serious, how she's been shooting everything in sight, and how lately she's seemed surly, moody, as if planning something.

Although when Henry asks her—quite rationally—*what* exactly she thinks her mother *might be planning*, Cheryl can't bring herself to say.

Henry reaches through the windshield and squeezes her shoulder. "Look, Cher," he says, measuring his words like heavy stones. "Everybody deals with stuff in their own way. Your mother has hers. You've got yours."

You don't get it, Cheryl thinks, but says nothing. When speaking to men like Henry, she is often aware of saying too much, the words leaking out like a whining, girlish song he'd turn off quick if it came on the radio.

"Your mom out back?" Henry asks, scanning the house. "We don't have all morning!"

He makes his voice sound jovial. Cheryl can't stand it, the idea of waiting by the side of the truck as her mother makes her tired way across the lawn, impersonating her father's gait, watching Henry pretend that everything is normal.

And yet all this only confirms that the plan is necessary. No one will believe her. She has only herself to rely on.

She runs down Boyer Street as fast as she can. She doesn't turn until she reaches the vacant lot where the boys sometimes play football in the warmer months, where she hides behind the trunk of a sycamore to catch her breath. She waits for almost an hour, long enough to be sure that Henry and her mother have left and that the house will be empty when she gets back. She has patience.

CHERYL WALKS BACK SLOWLY, using trees as cover, in case something odd has happened; she's relieved to discover the driveway empty and the house quiet. From the driveway, looking back toward the shed, the view through the window frightens her; she thinks a person is standing in the window, dark face craning toward the glass.

It's only the winch and hook from which the carcasses hang during butchering. She's never liked the shed, even if it is empty, the bloodstains on the floor.

She walks up to the front of the house and hears, in the distance, the call of a mourning dove. She has a mourning dove now—her most prized bird, which she caught with a trap on the roof outside her room and carefully shuffled inside. It doesn't call now, in captivity, which makes Cheryl sad.

There are storm clouds moving across the marsh, coming in off the bay, as Cheryl walks through the first floor, closing windows, though she would like to hear the rain beading the screens. She repeats this process on the second floor. In her mother's room she notices the bed is disordered, sheets humped on one side, as if someone were sleeping. She hits the bed with her hand, checking—no one there. She thinks about making the bed, but the idea makes her angry. She's nobody's wife!

She closes the windows in her mother's room, and then she goes up into the attic—which is hot, even in November, and smells of dust and cardboard—only to find that the one window up there is already closed.

Cheryl takes the cages from her room, the ones she's rigged up from the crab traps you can buy at the marina, bolstered with zip ties. The birds look ragged, confused by the light. She's been cruel, keeping them locked up so long.

Cheryl takes the cages into her mother's room, one by one. Once they're assembled, she removes the sheet from each one and opens the latches. The finch bolts immediately, chirping and fluttering madly around the room, searching for an exit. Cheryl worries that she might brain herself against a window, the way cardinals sometimes do, tricked by their reflection.

It settles on the bedspread at last, beside the humped-up blanket.

The others are tentative. The fat mourning dove is so still Cheryl wonders if it might be dead, but when she taps it lightly with a pencil, it ruffles its feathers and bobs away. "Take your time," Cheryl says. She decides to close the door behind her. Better to keep the carnage contained to one room, and anyway the bedroom is her mother's sacred space. Here she'll be most angry at the intrusion, most likely to retaliate.

By the time all the birds are set up in their staging grounds, the cages safely stowed in Cheryl's room, noon has already passed. Cheryl rests in the kitchen. She wastes an hour on her science homework—the delicate division of labor within a cell—but feels too restless to really concentrate. Her mother and Henry will be back toward evening, before the light fades. The exact hour depends on their patience. That leaves her a few more empty hours, at least—and yet she can't risk being in the house, in case their day ends early.

So she leaves the room, walks down the stairs, and goes down Boyer Street again, just as she would if she were heading to the general store to buy groceries for tonight's dinner. But she hasn't even gotten as far as the abandoned lot when the sky begins pouring rain. The temperature drops suddenly; even as Cheryl runs she feels herself shivering. By the time she gets to the store, she's soaked to the skin. Mrs. Edwards looks her up and down.

"I got umbrellas," she says.

"Can I wait here awhile?" Cheryl asks. "Just until the rain stops?"

"You do what you like," Mrs. Edwards shrugs. "No skin off my back."

She sits at the small interior table and watches the water run in rivulets into the gutters. She thinks of the birds bleeding through the house, trying to fly on battered wings, as her mother aims and fires. She smacks her forehead. *Stop it. Get ahold of yourself!*

Mrs. Edwards is behind the deli counter with a magazine. She isn't paying attention.

Eventually the rain stops. The lowering sun pools on the oily road as Cheryl walks down Boyer and turns up Wallingford, looking for Edna and Henry's place. It's getting dusky, the houses muddy in the fading light—but she recognizes the house from Halloween nights, when the two of them dress up like the Munsters, Edna dolled up like a vamp in a black dress and heavy makeup. But she didn't go this year, and their manicured lawn is already set for Thanksgiving, with paper cutouts of cartoon turkeys stuck into the soil.

Cheryl rings the bell. Is she really doing this? Is there no one else to turn to?

Edna comes to the door, brow furrowed with concern. "Cheryl, dear! What's the matter?"

"It's my mom," she says. "She's freaking out!"

She'd planned to fake tears, but now she finds they come unbidden; the hard part—after Edna rushes for her keys with eager steps, happy to be involved in a crisis—is making them stop.

Edna drives fast down Boyer, beeping at anyone foolhardy enough to cross the road. "Morons!" she says. "Emergency!" Cheryl shrinks down into her seat.

But when they get to the house, a surprise awaits: Henry's car is in the driveway. He stands next to it, arms crossed.

"Cheryl!" he yells, hands balled into fists. "Where the hell you been? I been looking for you. You went off like a shot before."

"I've been out."

"She came to see *me*," Edna says. "Said her mom was having some kind of a freak-out."

Henry narrows his eyes. "What game are you playing, girl?" he asks. "Your mother ain't even here."

"What do you mean?" Cheryl asks. "Didn't she go with you?"

"She never came out this morning," Henry says. "I knocked, even looked in the window. Then I thought I'd find you, ask what was happening, but you just ran off. Even went down to Stathem's Neck to see if your mom beat me there. You two went and wasted my whole day, you know that?"

His face is sour. Cheryl looks past him, stares at the house. Was her mother hiding, the whole time Cheryl set her trap? "I don't know *anything*," Cheryl says. "I've been out walking."

"This is ridiculous," Edna says, already nosing for secrets. "Let's just have a look inside."

The three of them walk to the door together. The two adults hang back and let Cheryl open it. She hesitates; what if her mother saw through Cheryl all along, and now she's waiting in the kitchen, ready to face these new intruders? But Cheryl never noticed her, even as she closed all the windows, up to the attic. Besides, she's gone too far to stop now. She wants Edna to see her mother with a gun, the bloody birds. She wants someone to understand her situation and sympathize.

She opens the door and finds silence, not even a coo. Cheryl is strangely disappointed. She's lived with this anxious silence too long.

"You checked out back yet?" Edna asks Henry.

"No," he says. "Didn't want to seem like I was snooping."

"Well, go now," Edna says. "Maybe she's just working there. Maybe she took a nap out back."

"That's not a place for naps," Henry says, but does as he's told.

Edna and Cheryl check the first floor—empty—before heading up the carpeted stairs. This time Edna goes first, unable to hide her growing interest, and Cheryl follows.

"That's my room," she says, when Edna tries the handle. "She's not in there."

Edna nods, and withdraws her hand. Cheryl's relieved. She'll hide the cages later, claim it was an accident. No one will blame her. "My mom's room is the far one," she says. Edna's already headed for her mother's door.

Easing it open, Edna snorts: it *does* look unclean. Again Cheryl notices the humped sheets from the morning, only changed, somehow: bigger, as if there might be a body underneath it. She gasps.

For that one moment—before Edna eases closer and taps the bed, as if to wake her sleeping mother—Cheryl has a vision which is really a wish: that her mother might be curled up in bed, asleep, just like her father always wanted to be on Saturday mornings, relieved of the burdens of husbandry. She imagines her mother sleeping so long that when she wakes she has no memory of hunting or of her father; her head will be purged of blood, and the empty space that remains will be filled with bad jokes and cheesy songs, the lemon light of afternoon streaming through the window. But this vision only lasts a moment before Edna breaks it.

"Bobbie Jean?" she asks, putting a hand on the nightstand to steady herself. "You sleepin'?"

The nightstand is lighter than she thinks, and the weight of her body tips it over, sending the alarm clock clattering to the floor. Edna curses, and from the other side of the bed, huddled for safety beyond the humped sheets, a gaggle of birds rushes upward: finch, sparrow, mourning dove. A chaos of wingbeats, battering the windows, mixes with Edna's screams.

BECAUSE OF THE CLOSED WINDOWS—not to mention the sound of Edna and the birds, overwhelming Cheryl's ability to hear, see, or even think—neither of them can hear the smaller sound Henry makes, a kind of strangled cry, standing before the shed window.

He will refuse to let Cheryl see. Children should be spared at least *some* things, and anyway she's had her share, this year. Is there any need to pile on more? People can only see so many things before breaking down. So he will argue to Cheryl, later, when she asks him *why*, and *how*, and *what exactly happened*.

He can't blame her for being frustrated—not because Henry doesn't mean well, but because he's no genius with words, and when he tries to tell her what he saw, he can't help admitting, even as he tries, that he can't come close to explaining.

The bare facts are easy. Her mother went back into the shed that morning, after Henry honked the horn and drove away but before Cheryl let the birds loose, sat in a chair with her lips around the barrel of a shotgun, and used her toe to pull the trigger. All that's clear from the coroner's report—clear to Henry, even beforehand. He knows about blast radius. He knows the specs.

But what he can never quite explain to Cheryl—despite

the many times she asks him to tell the story, calling him late at night, him and Edna, depending on who decides to pick up, as if the whole thing were somehow *their* responsibility—is the overall uncanny nature of the scene.

It was already a bloody place, with the saws and the hook where the carcasses had been hung. There were stains on the floors and trailing drops on the walls. A shotgun is messy, but so is a knife—especially when the person wielding it is a woman who's never done this kind of thing before, who is learning to do it out of a book. She should never have gone in that place, Henry thinks, though he won't say it, especially not to Cheryl.

She was lying where the deer might have lain, blown back, four limbs sprawled wide. Which animal was she? Who did those stains belong to, in the end?

Henry still gets a shiver, just thinking about it—lying in bed, his wife snoring, and this girl calling in the middle of the night, desperate to talk. She lives with her father's cousins now, up near Middletown. She has a new family to burden with her problems, and yet here she is, raving about how Middletown is nothing but cement—how she stays up all night, waiting for the daylight birds, but the mourning dove's is the only call she recognizes.

There ought to be a lesson in this, Henry thinks as he hangs up the phone, something about *roles*. Women with women, animals in their place. Never mix two kinds of blood.

ONE HUNDRED CHARACTERS
\\\\\\\\\

YOUR BROTHER, THE FIRST BOY you ever kissed. Your sister, the first girl your brother ever kissed. Your mother, who hasn't kissed anyone, to your knowledge, since the age of thirty-seven.

Your mother, a rebel in search of a cause. Your mother, a hurricane in search of an eye. Your mother, a crossword puzzle in search of one final long down solution that ends in X.

Your father, a miner, a prisoner of the system. Your father, a lawyer, a prisoner of the system. Your father, a governor, a prisoner of the system.

Your father, the captain of the HMS *St. Lucien of the Inner Isle*, married to the sea. The ship, his favorite child.

The sea, forever retracing its doom-laden portents. The sharks and their romantic hunger.

Your grandmother, born just before the war, the first female bail bondsman in New Canaan, Ohio, who, on her deathbed, refused to grieve, saying, "What are you all so *sad* about?" Your grandmother, born just after the war, the first female butcher in the town of New Jerusalem, Missouri, who, on her deathbed, was filled with inscrutable rage, saying, "I put my money in the mattress and left it for the junkman."

Your grandfather, trying to sleep. Your grandfather, almost asleep. Your grandfather, sleeping.

Your grandfather's dog, asleep. Your grandfather's dog, awake. Your grandfather's dog, speaking when your grandfather would prefer silence.

Your aunt, insane, living in great comfort in the Lauderdale Assisted Living Facility. Your aunt, insane, happily married with three children. Your aunt, insane, coming to knock at your door every three months, calling you by your brother's name, Jim. Your brother, Jim, the favorite, dead in a car accident. Your brother's name, Jim, as if he were still alive, each time it leaves the mouth of your aunt, insane.

Your uncle, eccentric, hiding the sugar after sunset in one of the seventy-nine rooms of his Westchester mansion, creating a purposefully inscrutable map leading to its hiding place, and then drinking himself into a blackout so that in the morning he will have a purpose to distract himself from the succession of empty hours.

Your uncle, normal, born with the moon in Cancer, unavailable in times of emergency.

Your family, scattered to the seven continents by fear and economic necessity. Your family, tethered like a button to the small logging town of Mulberry Hill, Saskatchewan.

Your family, a band of traveling minstrels. Your family, a band of traveling accountants. Your family, a mathematical equation with you as a remainder.

THE MAILMAN, dissatisfied with his route. The plumber, dissatisfied with your pipes. The landlord, dissatisfied with your financial situation.

The bus driver, concerned with the minutes. The passengers, concerned with the minutes. The people on the street, watching their minutes passing in the form of a bus, on its way to someone else's life.

The one-armed man on the bus with the sky-blue eyes. The long-legged child on the bus whom no one can control. The fair-haired woman on the bus whose face has been remade after a disfiguring accident, so that she is one person up close and another far away.

The friend who is waiting for you at the end of the line with a package of condoms and a letter from a former lover.

YOUR FRIEND, a shell-shocked success. Your friend, an outgoing failure. Your friend, a one-woman Rube Goldberg machine of unmitigated chaos in the form of an Italian girl from Northeast Philly with a masters in fine arts and a certification in small-business management.

The friend you lost to learning. The friend you lost to

romance. The friend you lost to the bright white nights of the Alaskan summer.

Your friend, a whiskey bottle. Your friend, a Brazilian python. Your friend, a math equation that no one will ever be able to solve. Your friend, imaginary.

Your childhood friend from South Philadelphia who made good. Your childhood friend from South Philadelphia who almost made good but was exposed as a criminal. Your childhood friend from South Philadelphia who made good, was exposed as a criminal, redeemed himself in the eyes of the people, and on the day of his death was carried in lamentation down Broad Street in a dark oak coffin for the thousand mourners to gnash their teeth and tear their hair in the presence of past glory.

Your childhood friend from South Philadelphia who slipped away from all these expectations and lived only for himself, only to be seized, late in life, by a feeling of foreboding, as if a heavy hammer were hanging over him and everything he cared about. Your childhood friend from South Philadelphia who goes to every length to pretend he is from Northern California. Your childhood friend from South Philadelphia who hates you with a passion and is working every day to discover your whereabouts in the hopes of exacting revenge.

A BOY IN CHINA with whom you once corresponded in an International Peace Pen Pal exchange, to whom you opened your heart with disturbing ease. A girl in Senegal whom you adopted through an International Children's Foundation, only to abandon a few months later because of personal financial distress. The cat in Japan, considered the very cutest of all the cats in the entire world—according to his owner—of whom you have become a fan on the Internet.

April, like the winner of a national talent search contest. August, like the inevitable failures of the government. February, like a life spent in Catholic educational institutions, so that you can hardly believe it when the first spring leaves hang down like bright skirts in the breeze.

THE MAYOR, ASLEEP. The police commissioner, drinking chamomile tea in his basement kitchen at four a.m. The district attorney, rubbing her husband's shoulders. The city comptroller, chewing his nails down to tiny barbed nubs as he watches the smiling girls with rosy cheeks circling Riverside Rink in the last icy atmosphere of early spring. The transit union president, chewing his cigar under the green hanging light that swings above a poker table.

The man who lives in the underground tunnels near City Hall who, if you believe him, has been mayor for thirty years and who will tell you, if you ask, exactly how many homeless people there are in the city and how, as mayor, he weeps for the fact that he has no power to feed and clothe them, due to the shortsighted policies of the city council and their backbiting ways.

THE PRESIDENT, patting your back. The vice president, flashing his insincere smile. The secretary of the treasury, seducing you at the hotel bar, despite your better instincts.

YOUR LOVER, asleep and dreaming of Mexico. Your lover, asleep and dreaming of Berlin. Your lover, asleep and dreaming of his former lover. Your lover, asleep and dreaming of the person she worries you used to be. Your lover, asleep and dreaming of the version of you of whom you are jealous.

The cowboy that reminds you of your lover. The Indian that reminds you of your lover. The damsel caught in the hand of the giant gorilla that reminds you of your lover. The lover that reminds you of the first four notes in Shostakovich's opus 110, the String Quartet in C Minor, that he wrote while living under the constant threat of imprisonment by the Soviet secret police.

Your ex-lover, listening for the hundredth time to the ending of the third movement of Charles Ives's *Three Places in New England*, who tells you, "Listen, here is the part where the chorus rises up and everything is explained," and to whom you say, "I'm sorry, but I've never been all that into classical music."

Your grandmother, living in another woman's body under the great, blank sky of Billings, Montana.

Your grandfather, that jowl-faced dog of a man, who discovered the cure for aging and lurks in the muck by the Four Creeks Central Reservoir.

Your uncle, stricken with amnesia. Your aunt, stricken with pleurisy.

Your cousin, who fell asleep at the wheel and woke up in a green valley, trapped in the crumpled frame of his wrecked jalopy while the birds gave throaty calls and the smell of cut grass slipped through the cracks in his windshield. Your cousin, the one with the theory about the transmutation of souls.

Your father, asleep. Your lover, asleep. You, awake, wondering if sleep will ever come.

YOUR STREET, ROLLING. Your car, diffident. The plane you are riding in, heedless of your fear. Your stewardess, fluent in several languages.

The sky above your house, laid flat, as if asking to be touched. Your house, painted blue, as if it could melt into the sky.

Your life, so full of people you can hardly believe it will ever end.

ASSASSINS
\\\\\\\\\

IN THIS CITY there are four assassins. Nobody knows their identities except the Bureau. They board crowded elevators. They are sometimes late with their utility bills. They open up cartons of eggs in the dairy aisle to check for cracks. They are meant to be perfectly invisible.

The assassins have not met each other. Assassin A operates in the leafy northwest corner of the metropolis, where the river valley rolls upward into foothills that are almost the suburbs. He is something of a homebody and rarely leaves his quadrant.

Assassin B handles the patchwork neighborhoods in the southwest: the Irish and Polish, the Ecuadorian. He has no business in the southeastern part of the city that Assassin C patrols: the Garment District, Little Italy, and Cedar Hill. What reason would he have to board an evening commuter train with Assassin A?

This is a city of neighborhoods, self-sufficient, balkanized. Everyone keeps to his own corners. Consider the northeast: a mysterious place full of converted warehouses, Korean grocers, and elevated tracks that keep the sidewalks dark. Why would Assassin C stroll there on a summer evening, until the blue sky disappears behind metal and broken glass crunches beneath his feet? This is the home of the mysterious Assassin D.

The Bureau monitors the assassins. Every night they are required to place a phone call to an unlisted number and give a ten-digit access code. After the code is entered, each assassin hears a series of three low tones. Assassin C—a passionate amateur cellist—has identified them as an E-major triad with the fifth in the bass and the third in the treble. Assassin A always feels extreme tension when he enters his code and a sense of relief when the chimes answer back. He fears making a mistake, although he never has.

If this call is not made, the assassin is considered Breached. A Breached assassin is subject to immediate assassination by the other assassins. For just such an emergency, each of the assassins is in possession of a dossier that contains pictures of the other three assassins and a list of vital information: height, weight, hair, and eye color.

If the assassins were to meet one another, however unlikely, they have been given strict orders to avoid interpersonal contact. For example, Assassin A is fairly sure he saw Assassin C on a downtown train one Friday night; he felt a rush of familiarity as the other man reached up to scratch his nose. He wanted to speak but remembered his training. He turned to the window and watched the giant dome of the golden Greek Orthodox church slip into the distance. He acted as if his fellow assassin were invisible.

As the assassins age, grow their hair, cut their hair, gain and lose weight, the other assassins receive periodic updates in the form of new photographs for their dossier. The assassins never receive their own photos.

Assassin A is uncomfortable with this. He stands at the station in a new suit and wonders who might be lurking nearby, taking his picture. Are they in the trees? Are they waiting in the far bushes with a high-powered lens?

When he receives his photographs, he studies them intently. *That's an odd haircut you've got there, B*, he thinks. He decides that C's mustache is a good fit.

He notices, over the years, that Assassin D never changes. They've worked together—if one can use that term—for over a decade now, and D has never once varied his appearance. He wears the same sunglasses and the same black jacket in winter and summer. He is the perfect image of an assassin: alone and unknowable. Perhaps he is from some ruthless Russian satellite nation.

EVERY MORNING Assassin A rides the 8:23 train to the very edge of his quadrant, walks to a tall slate-gray building, rides the elevator to the twentieth floor, and enters his small office. The pale yellow room is empty except for a Chagall print, a bookshelf full of books on the cinema, and a number of verdant potted plants.

Assassin A avoids making friends. He does not trust himself to keep enough space between his secret work and his desire to speak deeply to people. He is round and doughy, his voice sensitive. People trust him, but he cannot return the favor. Consequently, he adores small talk. He speaks warmly to the train conductor.

Assassin A has learned to anticipate the schedules of certain businesswomen and secretaries. He smiles shyly in their direction, apologizes for stealing the cream. *I would stay longer*, he thinks, *but my suit is a sham, and the things I do are secret.*

Once, when dining at the Il Grappa, a young waitress dropped a tray next to his table and began to cry.

"I'm so stupid," she told him.

The management led her away.

Later, after dinner, he saw the waitress out in the alley, by the dumpster.

"Do you have a light?" she asked. A strand of hair fell out of her ponytail and hung in front of her face as she shook the lighter. "I need this job."

Only with great difficulty did he avoid taking her in his arms and confessing: "I understand. I am an assassin."

Riding the 6:41 train home, he found himself near tears. The grid of the city was cold and definite as it passed beyond the window.

At time like these, Assassin A takes refuge in the movies. He is especially fond of the sort of foreign film that takes a slow, naturalist perspective on other people's lives. He likes the long, still shot of a knife cutting through a foreign fruit, the pan through the marketplace, the camera that follows a young woman as she crosses a cobblestone street.

Here is Assassin A in the final minutes of a spy thriller. It is a matinee; he is alone in the theater. The darkness swaddles him. The onscreen agent turns a corner with his gun held next to his ear. A string quartet scratches in the left channel as an engine starts in the background. The agent turns. Assassin A holds his breath.

Sixty feet, he thinks. *Drop and roll.*

He merges with the screen, and only when the lights come up does he remember once again where he is.

ASSASSIN B IS a committed volunteer. He works at the Overbrook soup kitchen on Tuesdays and the Shady Grove shelter on Thursdays. He practically runs the Clean Streets Litter Removal campaign, and he has given hours of manpower to the renovation of a number of trash-infested lots in Lower Richmond. On Sundays he takes long walks through the flourishing gardens, waving to the other volunteers, and thinks: this is time well spent. He wears worn black jeans over his rangy body and a red handkerchief around his sunburned neck. He still looks twenty-five, ten or so years after the fact. His hands are calloused, and he drinks a quart of water every hour.

He lives in a small brick row house next to an abandoned flavoring factory. The lighting is magnificent, and the rooms are spacious. He heats the apartment with a wood stove, and in the winter the warm air pools and swells the joists.

Assassin B shops responsibly. He enjoys local cherry tomatoes and organic sausages. He works his shift at the local co-op. Of the money he receives monthly he strives to donate half to charitable causes. He is concerned about the situation in Darfur, in Myanmar, in New Orleans.

He struggles to love his neighborhood, the corner stores and crumbling houses, but sometimes when he sits on his stoop, addicts accost him for money. If he gives it, they come back the next day and ask for more. If he doesn't, they call him stingy. He reminds himself that addiction is a disease, that economics are a factor, that oppression is the root of all evil, but sometimes, after they leave, he sits and stares at the strangers that pass his door. Everyone is foul-mouthed and malformed, unworthy of grace.

On nights like this, Assassin B begins to drink. Sometimes he finds himself out on the streets, long past midnight, looking up at the moon. Sometimes he sees a young man walking alone and follows him, at a distance of roughly one hundred meters.

Assassin B has superb eyesight; he can see the strong muscles in the young man's shoulders, the way his hips swing slightly as he walks. The young man meets up with other similar youths, standing on street corners, and Assassin B drops back; the danger of being seen is too great.

Some nights he is luckier. The young man meets no one he knows; he slips down a side street, then into the entryway of a tenement. The second floor window fills with light. Maybe the curtains are drawn, and Assassin B can only lean against a lamppost and imagine what goes on behind them. Or maybe they are open, and Assassin B can hide in the shadows and watch the young man stretching, doing pull-ups, preparing for bed.

Assassin B lines up the shot. It only takes a manner of seconds; he is experienced. He is not distracted by a passing car with booming subwoofers, by a woman screaming desperately for Anton, by a dog barking crazily behind razor wire. But he would never pull the trigger, faced with the ripe target of the young man's close-cropped head.

Not you, Assassin B thinks. You will be spared.

ASSASSIN C IS a patron of the arts and a member of the Cedar Hill Community Strings. There are so many places to be seen in the southeast corner of the city, so many poetry readings, rooftop cabarets, and progressive costume parties. Assassin C seems to be everywhere at once.

On Friday he goes to the City Opera production of Verdi's *Falstaff*, where he sits with the chairperson of the new Arts Avenue Development Initiative and discusses city council funding and capital campaigns. The opera house is far from full. The tenor lead is a bit weak in the high notes. The conductor left San Francisco in disgrace. What a pity it is that there are so few artistically minded people in this city!

Assassin C is a large and gregarious man. He has a happy excess of comforting fat around his middle, and his facial hair is thick and grandfatherly. Rumor goes around that he is the beneficiary of a large trust fund, that he is originally from Germany—is there a trace of an accent?—and that he is the mysterious restaurant reviewer whose identity is kept secret from the public.

His solo performance of Bach's Third Cello Suite once reduced a room of Cedar Hill matrons to silent tears.

Assassin C does nothing to dispel these rumors. He is fully aware of the reciprocal relationship between public and private personas. He never stays longer than an hour at any party. Already Cedar Hill is full of taxicabs, roof lights winking like amorous insects.

Before he leaves, Assassin C goes to the bathroom to freshen up. If the reflection in the mirror seems empty, lacking in sincerity, Assassin C reminds himself that this world is not his home. Every party is the same: clean lines, black dresses, and the cool smell of expensive perfume. If it weren't for the processions of clothes, the delicate brush-strokes on the Old Masters, and the occasional intrusion of gentle music, Assassin C might find himself giving up on humanity.

THE OTHER ASSASSINS WONDER how Assassin D spends his time. What is there to do in the Northeast? Who lives there? One finds nothing but miles upon miles of abandoned shipyards and weed-strewn brownfields, devoid of light. Assassin A imagines him sitting in an empty room, polishing his gun, shining his boots, sharpening his knives.

THE ASSASSINS RECEIVE their orders only twenty-four hours in advance. In the beginning they were inexperienced and had to scramble. It took time to prepare sight lines and survey mail routes. Their minds were laced with anxiety and occupied with floor plans and freight elevators. Jobs were done at the last possible second, with whatever tools were at hand. Luck was a factor.

Now the assassins are seasoned. They have time to prepare their personal rituals. Assassin A waters his lawn by twilight; the serenity of falling water soothes his disordered nerves. Assassin B makes himself a strong pot of tea, which he brews with ginger, lemon juice, agave nectar, and cayenne pepper, and rereads *The Wretched of the Earth*. Assassin C drinks Armagnac and plays Shostakovich's Cello Concerto, to steel his courage.

Moving in society circles, Assassin C prefers the subtle gambit. He has access to catered trays and private boxes. He has the opportunity to lean in and whisper. He is very good at laughing at just the right second to cover up other obtrusive sounds.

Assassin B has an aptitude for stealth and lives in an area where police response is poor. His neighbors respect his self-sufficient privacy. He has learned various ways of triggering explosives from remote locations. He knows where the roofs overlap.

As for Assassin A, who would suspect him? It is surprising that he is capable of even the smallest of crimes. He passes the checkpoints with ease. He seems to stumble into secret rooms. And yet he is capable of so much.

He is used to seeing faces frozen in surprise, that accusatory panic: *You?*

Yet no matter their methods, all the assassins experience hesitation from time to time. There are questions, lingering doubts. Isn't there some other way things could have turned out? When I was younger, maybe, perhaps in college. If I had lived abroad. If my parents had stayed together, or if they'd split up. If I'd experienced more or less heartbreak.

But when the gun sits cooling on the balcony, wiped of fingerprints; when the commotion is over and the police tape is wrapped around the telephone poles; when the door is closed to keep the painful whispers hidden from the lolling sound of chamber music, and the assassin steps back out into the open air, passing strands of speech and gentle waves of street commotion, it seems like such a little thing. How many years have they lived in this city, and what percentage of it has been spent in the dark? One night a month, two hours a night, one minute in an otherwise normal hour. Already the memory is beginning to fade. They pass horse-drawn carriages, ceremonial dinners, children bending at impossible angles in their pale pink leotards and crowns.

One cannot let his job define his life.

AFTER A MISSION, Assassin B regularly volunteers at a program that provides books for prison inmates. Assassin C locks the door of his apartment, takes his phone off of the hook, and reads one of his many biographies of the great German composers: Brahms, Beethoven, Mahler.

Assassin A struggles with insomnia. Once he hears the familiar three-note motif—the Bureau confirming the success of his mission—he hangs up the phone and begins writing a confession. All his confessions are contained in sixteen marble notebooks, titled "My Working Life." He keeps them in his locked lower desk drawer. His dream is that someday—perhaps after he is dead—they will be discovered and published, and someone will buy the movie rights. Assassin A also keeps track of his moviegoing in a separate series of marble notebooks, each entitled "My Life at the Movies."

All three assassins keep their guilt to themselves. They remember the steely expression of Assassin D, calm and untouchable, and they are ashamed.

ONE SUMMER, a visiting Georgian dignitary spent the night in a newly built hotel on the edge of the northeast quadrant of the city. He was surrounded by bodyguards, ensconced in a secure room, monitored by cameras, and ringed with complex security procedures. Yet he died in his sleep, somewhere around two in the morning. The official cause was sleep apnea.

Assassin A read about it in the paper. Assassin B overheard rumors while pulling weeds. Assassin C was privy to the whispers over tea at Space 36. But they all knew immediately that Assassin D had struck.

Even as they age and worry, fighting away remorse, Assassin D seems only to grow in skill. He is a master of poisons. He changes shape at will. He can climb sheer vertical walls like a spider.

Assassin D seems to exist in the territory of their dreams and nightmares. His powers are not limited by physical laws.

IT IS THE SECOND WEEKEND in September. For weeks the city has been experiencing the kind of heat wave that comes with an Indian summer. Everyone complains. How could we have been so stupid to settle in such a stolid, swampy place? The gray clouds never lift, and we are troubled by swarms of mosquitoes.

Then, on Saturday, a cool breeze sweeps in from the west. A thunderstorm catches Assassin B at the Lower Richmond Community Center. He is waiting for the bus in the new air when his phone blinks, indicating a message.

Assassin C is at an impromptu gathering in Mrs. Q's loft. Mrs. Q says she would have gotten away more often to the house in Maine, but her activities on the Waterfront Planning Committee have occupied so much of her time. Assassin C is eyeing the bottle of Booker's on the far table in quiet desperation when the message arrives.

"I am so sorry," he tells Mrs. Q. "Someone's dragging me to Queen Street."

The tip of his mustache quivers imperceptibly.

Assassin A has fallen asleep watching three episodes

of a popular cable crime drama. One of the characters has a slight scar on her lip, and Assassin A dreams briefly of touching it, of asking where she received it, of sharing sad stories of childhood. The phone in his pocket vibrates, and his dreams take a strange turn; he is walking on a long tightrope stretched between two large towers, and a brass band is waiting to strike up a Souza march. Someone is creeping along the wire beneath him, silently, hand over hand.

AS SOON AS ASSASSIN B returns home he begins to drink and rearrange his furniture. He drags tables across the floor and upends couches. He grows tired, but the room is still wrong. There is no place comfortable to sit anymore.

Assassin C admits to a certain agitation, but he tells himself he is not surprised. It was inevitable that this day would come. He climbs to the roof of his condo complex with his cello and plays Bach under the stars. It gives him temporary confidence.

Assassin A receives the message much later than the others. He wakes up in the morning feeling displaced, his face pressed into the couch cushions. His phone blinks. He reads the message, stumbles out on the lawn, and collapses beneath the cheerful morning sun.

When he wakes, he is surprised and frightened to find that he is still alive. He brightens up: maybe it was only a dream! But there it is, the message, still on his phone: Assassin D is Breached.

THE DIRECTIVES IN THIS SITUATION are clear and un-
ambiguous. All other activities are to be suspended until
the Breached assassin has been dealt with. Each assassin
must act alone. Their identities cannot be compromised. So
each makes his own plans, fully aware of the undeniable
fact that Assassin D is working too, planning their deaths
down to the last detail.

Assassin C is not afraid. He knows that grappling with
Assassin D on his terms is a pointless exercise. He finds
himself looking forward to meeting the mystery man. It
has been a long time since there was a test of his abilities.

He decides not to cancel any social obligations. He at-
tends a party at Madam P's, at the western penthouse of
Cedar Hill Towers. He will not be detained.

Madam P's party is somewhat dreary. There are not
enough young people to incite libelous talk. Assassin C is
about to leave when an unknown hand slips a note into
his pocket. Startled, Assassin C turns around, but finds no
one. The note reads: *Leaving so soon?*

Someone is playing a practical joke on him. Only
slightly shaken, Assassin C partakes of the tapenade. He
rehangs his coat, embarrassed. People note his lingering
presence with approval. He is bumped near the coat closet.

"Excuse me."

He turns around to meet the speaker, but no one is
there. A lady in a black mini-dress watches him from the
corner. Laughing, she covers her mouth with her hand.
There is another note in his pocket. *Stay awhile.*

Assassin C takes a shot of Booker's. People begin to leer

at him. He snarls at a man in a tweed coat who is taking up more than his fair share of floor space.

"Give me some room, for chrissake. Don't crowd me."

"No one's crowding you, darling," Madam P replies in a thin voice.

He apologizes, but to his great embarrassment he slurs his words. The Madam is displeased. He would like to go to the bathroom to freshen up, but such actions are suicidal. Avoid closed spaces. Survey the exits.

The guests are all leaving. Madam P. is giving him his coat. "Time waits for no one," she says, and laughs.

He is laughing too, a little too loudly. Can't he stay a little longer? He is dead on his feet.

No one else is laughing.

"Let me call you a cab," Madam P says, but does not dial a number. He can see her pretense, but he cannot protest. He is being shuffled out the door. Can it be possible that he is the last person at the party?

There is the hall, and the elevator. Its mouth opens. Like a true drunk, he stumbles into the metal box. He looks for the cameras, stupidly. Anyone with any intelligence would already have cut the video cable.

He tries to think of some way he could have prevented all of this. He could have stayed home, he could have locked the door, he could have sat on the couch with his Luger pointed a little above the knob. His throat dries out. One minute he is breathing, and the next his trachea is dry as sandpaper. The lights in the elevator go out, and there is a small sound like a pencil breaking through paper.

ASSASSIN B HAS NOT SLEPT longer than an hour for almost a week now. His days and nights are taking on a gapped quality. Minutes will go by in total blankness. Small sounds—the settling of the house, his own heart-beat—seem unnaturally enlarged, as if everything were being amplified by hidden microphones.

He is following a boy again. He has seen him during the day from his window as he sits, cleaning his gun. The boy is a little over six feet tall and past the edge of seventeen. He loiters on the stoop with his friends, joking and some-times fighting each other. Sometimes mothers come along and scream at them, and they scatter like rain. He wants to scatter along with them.

One night, Assassin B dropped down the fire escape and followed the boy to where he lives, a small apartment near the tracks where the Citrus Express runs, bearing or-anges. The train came and rattled the tracks, rattled the house, rattled the window where the boy was standing, watching it.

Assassin B's behavior is reckless. Something attracts him to the boy. He talks less than his friends. He watches the Citrus Express as it flies by his window. There is some magic in the relation of his long, lean body to the machine howling under him.

Why did Assassin B ever give his life to the Bureau? Maybe in the beginning he believed in justice, but it didn't take long for its hypocrisy to become apparent. What sort of noble system could put a gun into the hands of Assas-sin B, as if its ends justified all means? He belongs with the boy, with the people.

Assassin B is drunk all the time now, is drunk every time he slips down the drainpipe like a criminal and crosses alleys toward the dark spot where this boy's window is visible.

Again he goes to McLaughlin's. The bartender is the owner's niece. She pours long and purrs endearments. Somebody is playing jazz on a jukebox that has never played jazz before; the music sings in a minor key on the verge of collapse. Just as he is losing consciousness, he becomes aware of the boy against his right shoulder.

"Would you like a cigarette?" the boy asks.

The man from the Bureau is watching him, feeding the jukebox, waiting for him to make a mistake.

Out in the street, Assassin B is afraid again.

"I have some money," he says.

The boy leads him down a back alley. "I know a place."

His jaw is outlined by the periodic streetlights. Assassin B feels like an old man in the hospital with a terminal illness watching a young nurse cutting bandages. How did he grow so old?

Lying in bed in the top room of the boy's house, Assassin B is completely vulnerable. His gun is in the corner, discarded with his clothes. He stands there watching the boy as the boy looks upward at the moon in the middle of the sky. His body is outlined by the window. Maybe the world is less cruel than he thought.

The Citrus Express rattles. The moon is gibbous and yellow. Late crickets stutter in the grass.

A gun fires, muffled by the silencer. Glass shatters; the boy is hit.

Now Assassin B is on his feet. He can't look at the boy lying on the floor. He looks at the end car of the Citrus Express trailing away under a far railway bridge. Everything is my fault, he thinks. My conscience has caught me.

Across the street, in the abandoned building that was once the Crawford Ball Bearing factory, a barrel glints in the moonlight.

ASSASSIN A IS NOT SURE if he has gone insane or if the world is simply full of light. He spends most days in his garden. The sun burns his skin, and he sweats beneath his bathrobe. The Beretta is cool against his flesh.

At night he dreams the same dream he had as a child: a monster behind a door, breathing heavily. But when he flings open the door, the monster has vanished. There is nothing but a stone walk, a red lamppost, and waving sycamores. His phone blinks a message. Assassin C is down. Assassin B is down. Commence operations.

He wakes before dawn and prepares his escape. He showers and applies a new face. He dresses himself in a button-down Hawaiian shirt. He conceals the gun. He selects a pair of Ray-Ban sunglasses and sport sandals. By the time he is done, it is almost dawn, and he looks like a completely different person. The sprinklers are chittering in the gray air.

Assassin A steps onto the commuter train. It switches at Foxboro Junction and makes a circuit of the city. In the southwest the traditional Abdication Day is gearing up; the Ecuadorians are hoisting tent poles and assembling a giant snake puppet to disgorge the souls of the iniquitous. As the train lingers in Callowhill Station, Assassin A imagines the ghost of Assassin B boarding the train, lingering in a frontward seat, shimmering and fading.

Brother, he thinks—*I hardly knew you.*

In the southeast, all is sedate. From the occasional open window, he hears placid lull of public radio. Jade plants and dogs appear in the windows. A mother leans cooing over a baby. Assassin C no longer lives here.

A long brick wall shunts everything into silence: Willard Station. So far Assassin A has not seen any agents. Still, he tries as best he can to mix with the crowd. One never knows who might be in the employ of the Bureau. He buys a business-class ticket for the southbound train to Atlanta, using one of his many doctored government IDs.

He sits down in one of the spacious chairs and leans backward. The train begins to pull out of the station, and Assassin A feels a sense of elation like nothing he has experienced before. He pulls out the seventeeth volume of "My Working Life"—the other sixteen volumes are stowed in his suitcase—and prepares to write the last entry of his masterpiece.

A man sits down across from him just as he opens the marble notebook. Assassin A looks up and is shocked. The man is wearing the same gray suit Assassin A wears on Tuesdays and a blue-striped Brooks Brothers shirt, much like one that he himself owns. Even the man's hairstyle is similar to his; a left-side part, a fringe of hair that falls across the forehead. Only the eyes and the hard, prominent nose betray the newcomer: Assassin D.

The resemblance is uncanny. Assassin D has even lightened his skin to imitate Assassin A's own unpleasant, doughy complexion. Assassin A cannot help admiring the thorough workmanship.

Without pause, the two men reach for their guns, concealing the barrels beneath unfolded copies of Amtrak's *Trailways* magazine. The conductor comes by to check their tickets, nods, and moves onward.

The car is quiet. Assassin A is the first to speak, gun still trained on his companion. "Look. I don't want to kill you. I don't want to be man who shoots man who shoots man. I want out."

Assassin A is talking too quickly. He keeps his voice lowered. He has roughly thirty minutes until the next stop.

Assassin D does not even seem to register that someone else is speaking. He barely blinks. He keeps the gun level, whereas Assassin A's shakes, ever so slightly.

"It's like the game with the two men in a room who can't talk to each other, with the finger on the button. That's why the Bureau never wanted us to meet. Two men in two separate rooms; each of them has their finger on a button that can blow up the other one. Kill or be killed!"

Assassin D blinks a few times in rapid succession. Have Assassin A's words had some small effect on him? Or was it simply dust?

"But if we can talk to each other—if we can communicate!—then things are different. We don't have to go running for the button. We're both already Breached. The old directives don't apply."

Assassin D seems to be smiling. Assassin A can't quite

tell, but his upper lip is curling the slightest bit at the edge of his mouth. Assassin A studies the other man's parody of his own appearance. The pallid makeup makes Assassin D resemble a corpse. The whole picture is of a pathetic, sedentary person, but Assassin A can't say that it isn't a good likeness. His Beretta feels unnaturally heavy.

"What's the point of killing me?"

Assassin A points to his chest. His shirt is garish; his thumb touches a yellow palm tree. The lights flicker as the train clatters over a gleaming river.

"I'm a joke of an assassin. I get sweats. Everything I do is pretty much luck. I don't want to kill you! I don't want to kill anyone."

By now Assassin A is pleading. His voice makes inappropriate leaps in register.

"We don't have to push the button, like the Bureau tells us to. Even with a silencer, someone might hear. I'll be bleeding everywhere. Too many variables!"

Assassin D makes a small motion with his head. It could be a nod. It could be a twitch, a creak in a stiff neck. The conductor comes by again, laughing to himself. When he is gone, Assassin A leans in an inch and whispers.

"Last month I was standing in the station at Southwark. I'd just finished a mission. I was waiting to go home. And all of those people were just walking around, totally unaware. They didn't know I had a gun. I could have pulled it out and popped their heads off, one by one. I knew the exits."

Assassin D doesn't seem to be listening. He scratches his exceptionally well-defined nose.

"But these people were going home to their families.

Sitting ducks. I felt sick; so lonely I could have puked. I thought about putting the barrel to my head and blowing my brains out."

Now Assassin D seems intrigued. He is still sitting up very straight in his chair, but his head is cocked to the left side. He is staring right at Assassin A. Assassin A measures the level of emotion in Assassin D's implacable gray eyes.

"We're on a train. We're going somewhere, for the first time in forever. Just two people, taking a train to visit the relatives. Just talking, like the rest of humanity."

Assassin A feels extraordinarily tired. All the words have left him. Assassin D is truly smiling now. As Assassin A watches, he reaches his other hand—the one not holding the gun—all the way up to his hair and runs his fingers across his scalp. Set against Assassin D's practiced stillness, it seems a languid and extravagant gesture.

"Do you understand what I'm saying?"

Assassin D laughs a little. It's not an actual laugh, exactly, but the suggestion of a laugh, caught in his throat. And when the laugh is done, Assassin A notices a small tremor float across Assassin D's entire face, starting at his mouth and traveling up his left check to his eye. The tremor seems to confuse Assassin D's two faces, as if, for a brief second, Assassin D and his Assassin A disguise are merging, and the sallow skin and flabby paunch are not a matter of mockery, but something trapped inside Assassin D himself. Assassin D opens his mouth, still trembling, and speaks.

"Yes."

The word hangs there between them. It dangles like a

confession. The paper over Assassin D's Glock 17 rustles, a small, subtle motion. The barrel moves, barely an inch, but the implications for a bullet's trajectory are vast. It's a tiny mistake, but Assassin A sees it. He takes advantage.

First he lets out a giant, theatrical cough. Then he empties the barrel directly into Assassin D's heart. The silenced shot sounds like a quick burst of air.

Assassin D jerks in his seat, goes limp. Assassin A takes the gun from Assassin D's fingers and puts it in his luggage. He puts the Amtrak *Trailways* magazine over the bullet hole. He leans back in his seat.

Assassin D's face stares at him accusingly. The eyes bulge in shock. The makeup, along with the steely gray eyes—now frozen—have a grotesque effect: Assassin D's dead face is staring out from inside his Assassin A disguise like a man in a bear costume. Assassin A places his Panama hat over the other man's eyes.

The conductor comes by, whistling. He notices the two of them—the magazine and the hat.

"Is your friend sleeping?"

The conductor looks over Assassin D with unmistakable tenderness. The warmth in his eyes makes Assassin A so lonely that he can't speak.

He didn't lie to Assassin D. The train story, the two men in the room—he believed it. He tells himself that he had no choice. He takes out volume seventeen of "My Working Life." *I killed Assassin D*, he writes. Seeing the words on the page, he has to look away, out the window. A small trickle of blood creeps below the lower margin of the Amtrak *Trailways* magazine.

The train passes a billboard of a popular movie actress. Assassin A is heartbroken. He didn't want to kill Assassin D. Now that he is dead, he imagines the sort of conversations the two of them would have had. He imagines the two of them in a smoky café in some European city. The glasses clink, the band plays a lovely and anachronistic brand of jazz. They clink glasses, sip their Pernod. Together they bear the darkness.

The train conductor calls the next stop. In the ensuing commotion, Assassin A slips off of the train, wipes Assassin D's gun clean of fingerprints, and drops it in the division between train and platform. The sound as the gun hits the gravel is too small to be noticed, but to Assassin A it has a hollow ring, as if it has been falling for a long time in a soundless place. No one notices. Nobody looks at him. He has the strange sensation of merging into himself, like paper folding inward to form a picture that had previously been hidden. An air horn sounds. He would like for there to be violins. *I killed Assassin D*, he thinks. He walks down the platform to the central stairs, mindful of his gun, mourning his fallen comrades.

TINY CITIES MADE OF ASHES
\\\\\\\\\\

I REMEMBER THE ULLMAN BOYS: the six-man army, bristling with sticks, that colonized our narrow strip of Craydon Street. Every afternoon from half past three 'til dark, they filled the air with shouts of *C-A-R*, *game on*, and *pass the puck*, burly brothers who ranged in age from nine to seventeen but shared one face—flattened nose and eyes sunk back in their sockets. They were pug-ugly, built for hockey, grunting and hurling each other against the goals. They made the rest of us their audience.

One afternoon in September *the rest of us* was me and a kid named Trevor Hendricks. He sat on the grass in front of his house, skinny arms around his knees. We were in the same grade at school, along with ten other kids, and although I'd only been in town a month, I knew his name and face. From the worn green picnic bench outside the Elverton Mail Bag General Store, washing down my Sour Patch Kids with Coke, I watched Trevor watch the street. I sized him up. He looked lonely, or at least alone, and I thought: *Here is someone you could convince to be your friend*.

I went over to him. "You gonna watch this game all day?" I asked.

"I don't know." Trevor shrugged. "Maybe."

"Hey, fags," the Ullman boys yelled. "Get a room."

His shoulder blades shifted beneath his shirt, shaking off the insult.

"We could go to my house," he said. "If you want."

Nobody in Elverton had ever invited me over before. I hadn't invited anyone to my house either; my father didn't like visitors.

I followed Trevor quickly across the lawn, not wanting to give him time to change his mind, while the Ullman boys made kissing sounds behind us.

Trevor's mother sat on a torn couch in their living room, flipping through *National Geographic* and smoking furiously. She was a short and stubby woman. A housedress hid her hips. Clusters of teacups and dirty ashtrays covered the coffee table, and in the far corner, on top of a scarred upright piano, two stuffed muskrats stood frozen in midfight, fur spangled with ash.

"Nice to see a new face," she said.

"Let's go downstairs," Trevor said, tugging my arm. "Let's build something."

The basement floor was smooth concrete. Two small windows on the far side let in just enough light to see the metal shelves lining the walls, filled with screws and bolts. Trevor brought out a wooden crate of plastic building blocks, and we worked without speaking, fitting squares.

Trevor had long, nimble fingers. He could make a life-like roof out of slanted blocks, a credible window. All I could build was a one-story shack, but Trevor made something like a church: peaked gables and a high-tipped steeple.

"That's good," I said.

"It's *okay*. Wanna see something?" He pulled a model out from beneath the shelves.

On a large green square of pegged plastic, large as a foldout road map, buildings stood in two clean lines, an invisible street between them. Two structures broke the symmetry: a broad white box with three tall doors and a long red building, crowned by a cracker-flat roof.

"Whaddaya think?"

It looked like the view from a low-flying plane: square and lonely.

"We're here." Trevor pointed at a smaller house with more detail than the others. Through its front windows I could see a living room, and beyond that a smaller room with a half wall: a dining room and kitchenette. The walls were uniform gray. Only by looking hard could I see the tiny seams between the plastic blocks.

"What do you mean, here?"

"We're *here*," Trevor repeated, touching the roof.

Then I saw. The tiny house was Trevor's. The model was Craydon Street. The broad white building with three doors was the Elverton Volunteer Fire Department, and the little red building was our school, Elverton Elementary and Junior High, population ninety-six, stinking of milk and chalk.

"You can touch it, if you want."

I started at school and walked my fingers down the empty road, ticking off houses: *one, two, three.* I got to *eleven*, and there it was on the right: my house in miniature, white walls, two thin columns supporting a porch, a wide yard on the north side my mother filled with flowers.

Trevor's mother called, voice thick with tar. "Trevor! Come help me with dinner."

"Come back tomorrow," Trevor said.

"Have you shown this to anybody else?"

"No." He put the model back.

By the time I left, the late September sun was almost gone. The Ullman boys were packing up their goals, pulling PVC pipes from their hinges. The oldest one waved his stick at me. It looked tiny inside his thick hand.

"What'd you two do together?" he yelled. "Suck each other's dicks?"

I looked left and right down Craydon Street, the houses laid out just like Trevor's model. That was when I realized Trevor wasn't watching the Ullman boys at all. He was measuring the buildings.

THE NEXT DAY I STOOD by the rusted geodesic dome—which teachers warned us never to climb, for fear of tetanus—and watched kids kick Trevor around the playground. They choked his head inside their armpits and stripped his shoes off. I wanted to help him, but there was nothing I could do, small and solitary myself. I felt sorry for Trevor but envious too. Nobody touched *me* like that.

We walked home together afterward. Soybean chaff flickered in the fields. Bulbous squash grew wild in kitchen gardens.

"Nobody talks to me," I said.

"You're lucky," Trevor said.

That afternoon we spanned the town—Craydon, Bacon's Run, Market, and Ridgeway—measuring houses. Trevor ran his hands over the walls and window frames, fingers learning the shapes, while I stood by the edge of the road and took photographs with a camera my mother had bought *to encourage my interests*.

"We're historians," Trevor said. "They'll want to know what this town was like in a hundred years."

"We could give our model to the Historical Society," I suggested.

I liked the Historical Society, a low brick building with a red door that was once a bank. The old women who volunteered gave me candy, and I liked running my fingers over the old maps of Elverton, as if history were my personal possession.

"I don't like those people," Trevor said.

Trevor didn't like anybody, definitely not Mrs. Waddell, who ran the counter at the Mail Bag. She didn't let him go inside the store alone, and when he came in with me, she still wouldn't let him use the bathroom.

Maybe what we had wasn't quite a friendship—it was

just two boys taking measurements. I didn't have much to compare it to. My family followed my father from job to job, one nuclear plant after another: Calvert Cliffs, Peach Bottom, Indian Point. Not that we *lived* in any of these places—my father never used that verb. He was *supervising* at Peach Bottom; he was an *adviser* at Indian Point.

These kinds of linguistic distinctions were important to my father. He only recommended termination; he never actually *fired* anyone. He was not responsible. After the fat was trimmed and the streamlined plant passed inspection, he would be off again, faithful family following behind.

Only Elverton felt less temporary to me now, after months in Trevor's company. I knew the houses: paint peeling like birch bark in the sun, gabled roofs and gutters. I had pictures as proof. I put them in an envelope labeled *Evidence* and tucked them on his basement shelf beside our little city.

WE FINISHED THE MAIN SQUARE in November. A cold rain fell as Trevor made his final calculations. I stood at the corner of Market and Ridgeway and aimed my camera at our last house, an ugly two-story with vinyl siding and pale green sills. Just before I released the shutter, Trevor turned from his measurements, looked straight at the lens, smiled, and gave me a thumbs-up—a goblin with peaked ears and dry, yellow skin. There was no one home in the house behind him, but still I worried. How weird would we look to the people who lived inside?

The rain fell heavy as we walked back to Craydon. Even the Ullman boys had taken momentary shelter. Their silent goalposts dripped.

"What are we gonna do now?" I asked.

"More houses, I guess," Trevor said, but he seemed shifty about it, and I worried—not for the first time—that his future plans didn't include me and that for the rest of my time in Elverton I'd be left friendless, listening to my twin brothers argue over toys while my father paced the living room, rehearsing speeches.

"Can I come over for a bit?" Trevor asked.

This was a shock. Normally, I would have said no—my parents had specific rules about visitors—but the friendly gesture overwhelmed my defenses.

"Sure," I said. "Of course."

When we came through the door, my mother was at the kitchen table, paying bills. "Who's this?" she asked, harried.

The twins were at the table too, working on a jigsaw puzzle, but as soon as they saw Trevor, they lost interest and trained their eyes on the outsider. Hard to remember how *small* they were in those days, thin little children.

"This is Trevor," I said. "We'll just play Sega. We won't bother anybody."

"All right," my mother said, squinting. "But stay on the porch."

Our screened-in porch was empty, except for the former tenants' patio furniture and a blurry television with the Genesis attached. Trevor and I took turns playing

Sonic. There was only one controller; my mother disliked competition. Trevor was no good. The buttons stuck beneath his clumsy thumbs.

"We can play something different," I said. "If you want."

"Where's your bathroom?" Trevor asked.

"Past the kitchen," I said, and turned back to the screen.

I was so busy maneuvering through a world of flashing lights that I didn't realize how long he'd been gone. I was about to face the boss of Pinball Palace when my mother appeared, holding Trevor by the shoulder. Her face was red. "Next time tell your friend the right way to the bathroom."

"I *did* tell him," I said, focused on the screen.

"I don't like people sneaking around my bedroom!"

I paused the game. What was Trevor doing in my parents' bedroom, all the way on the second floor?

"I've got my hands full with dinner," my mother said. "Tell your friend it's time to go home." She walked away, letting the door slam.

Trevor was shaking, but his lips curled up into a guilty smile beneath his beaked nose. His eyes looked tiny. I remembered how Mrs. Waddell watched him when he walked into the Mail Bag and didn't let him use the bathroom.

"You better go."

Trevor slipped out the porch door and onto the rainy street, leaving me alone.

I stared at the frozen television. Pinball Palace seemed meaningless. My first Elverton friend, and I'd picked a weirdo, someone even my mother knew was defective.

Maybe my parents were right, and I *should* be suspicious of outsiders.

After a while my mother came back. "Sorry for being short. That boy has a history."

"A history?"

"Some women were talking at the Mail Bag," she said. "A teacher found him in the girls' bathroom at your school, hiding in the stalls. Not just once—several times."

I imagined Trevor in the girls' bathroom, arms crossed, sizing up its dimensions. What did this say about our project? After dark, when I was safe in bed, did Trevor sneak from house to house, opening windows?

"I know things are hard," my mother said. "This is your dad's tough year. He'll get a long-term position soon. Buckle down, buddy!" She mock-punched me in the arm. "We'll get through it."

That was my mother: the kind voice and the firm hand, good cop and bad. My father worked long hours, and when he was home, he spent most of his time in the office upstairs. Even before the trouble started, my mother was the only parent I had. At the end of that night's dinner, as we cleaned the last carrots from our plates, my father rolled up his sleeves and cleared his throat. He looked tense, as he often did those days—wiry, electric with nerves. The dark circles under his eyes gave his words extra gravity.

The three of us had it pretty good, he began. We were allowed to do the usual things kids did: soccer leagues, summer camps, spelling bees. We had all the opportunities. There was no reason for us to be unhappy—didn't we agree? He only asked one thing, that we keep our socializing *out of the house*. He had nothing against kids—in fact he liked some of them very much—but let one in and more would follow. Not just kids but their parents too, *plant employees*, wanting to talk and socialize and ask *questions*, and even if their parents weren't plant employees, then their uncles were, their aunts or their cousins, all of them with *questions*, all of them *curious*, and once you started talking, answering *questions*, they'd never stop asking, and how was he expected to do his job with people always *asking him questions*, as if he had answers, as if he could help them?

While he talked, our mother stroked his knuckles, trying to keep his hands still.

I GREW SIX INCHES that year. I proved my toughness on the kickball field, wrestling the rubber sphere out of the air and pegging the speeding runner's head. I won a grueling forty-foot race across the double monkey bars, linking my legs around another boy's hips and hurling him to the sand. When a tall kid told me his father said my father was a fag, I shoved his face into an anthill until he screamed.

One afternoon in April, a scuffle broke out by the geodesic dome. Boys crowded around in a tight ring, yelling, *fight, fight, fight*. I shoved into the circle. I was no shy kid anymore. People gave me room.

Trevor was lying in the middle, holding his stomach. The kid who'd been beating him was already turning away.

I took over. I put my foot on Trevor's neck.

"Long time no see," he wheezed.

Although I saw Trevor every day, I always looked past him. I didn't want people to remember we'd been friends.

The other kids chuckled. "Shut up," I told them. "Get out of here."

The teacher blew his whistle, and the crowd trickled away. Recess was over, but still I kept my foot on Trevor's throat, like he was a snake I couldn't risk letting go.

"You still sneaking around town?" I asked. "Looking in people's windows?"

Trevor smirked but didn't say anything.

"How's that model we built?"

"*You* didn't build anything," Trevor said, twisting up his mouth. "You're not a builder."

I took my foot off his neck and kicked him once in the ribs. The teacher didn't intervene. Nobody ever intervened when Trevor was involved.

"Get out of here," I said. I watched Trevor's back as he slunk away.

What did Trevor know about being a builder? I was building my own city now—a city of experience. Trevor wasn't invited to Alex Edward's fourteenth birthday party that May, but I was. As soon as I got in the front door, my hands ran over the banisters, measuring. The inside was clean and fresh, plush carpet and goldenrod walls. Trevor may have run his hands across those windowsills when the family wasn't looking, but he'd never been invited inside.

After the boys ate cake, we tramped out to the back-yard to play touch. Their lawn was as immaculate as their carpets, brushed clean of sticks and leaves. A sudden snap, and Stephen Ambrose, backup quarterback, flung the football at the back of my head. Maybe it was a mistake, but I didn't care. I turned and charged, hurling my body into his and pummeling away. It took six of them to pull me off.

While Alex's mother called my house with news of the fight, I sat on a solitary chair in that golden living room and listened to the adults whisper about my violent ways. I knew they'd never let me come back.

When I came home, I found my father had already called a meeting to discuss what I'd done. He had my mother and the twins around the kitchen table, their faces full of concern, but not for me. They were watching him as he paced erratically around the room, occasionally bumping against the handle of the refrigerator and the hard corners of the countertops, as if he couldn't be troubled by the details of the physical world.

He didn't *blame* me for what I'd done. If anything, he blamed himself—for introducing us to this sort of environment, in which *survival of the fittest* was the law of the land, in which *brute force* was the only language anyone understood. Didn't we see, then, how *crucial* it was that we not let ourselves be *unduly influenced* by this environment? Didn't we recognize the *sensitivity of the situation*? Hadn't he done his *absolute best* to protect us? And yet here I was, acting like a *hooligan,* fraternizing with the enemy!

We were used to these sorts of speeches, by that point. There was the *Pitch In Together* speech, the *Trust No One* speech, the *Sports Are a Distraction from the Real-*

ity of Life speech. There was nothing odd about my father giving speeches. His work was speeches: motivational speeches, procedural speeches, disciplinary speeches. But as the pressure grew—as it became clear that there was organized resistance to his safety regime, as the year mark passed and he failed to meet deadline after deadline— the hand gestures that accompanied these speeches became increasingly wild, like a loose piece of machinery, deformed by stress. He was moving too quickly around the room, pulling so aggressively on the piece of scalp directly above his forehead that large clumps of hair came off in his hands.

This time my mother made no move, either to comfort or to stop him. Maybe she felt she couldn't, trapped in a script she was powerless to alter. She only looked at me sadly, as if this was all my responsibility, as if I'd set the stage and started the scene in motion.

I GOT MY FIRST GIRLFRIEND that June: Amber Elwell. She lived at the edge of town, where Bacon's Run met Ridgeway, past soybean fields and stands of oak, past Wiskasset Creek, lined with stunted beech trees. I could only see her for an hour at a time, after school ended and before my mother got home from work; now that my father had taken a leave of absence from his job, my mother had gotten a position as a dentist's bookkeeper—"to keep our options open," she told us. But just because he wasn't allowed to go to the plant didn't mean my father's working days were over; he still spent much of his time in the attic, going over security procedures. He had no time for the twins, which meant that after school they were my responsibility.

But I was happy to shirk it, in service of a greater cause. Amber Elwell would change my reputation. I would prove to everyone that I was no vicious bully. I had the gentle hands of a lover.

One afternoon, lying red-faced on her living room couch, I heard Amber's dog barking outside. My heartbeat rang in my ears: her mother, home!

I crept to the window and looked out onto the lawn. Trevor was at the edge of the road, carrying binoculars. He didn't bother hiding them, and when he saw me, he smiled that particular half-smile of his, as if he was satisfied I'd been forced to look in his direction, despite all my efforts to ignore him.

Amber joined me at the window. "You creeper," she yelled. "My brother's gonna kill you!"

The window was open, and I knew Trevor could hear her shouts, but he didn't make a sign—just tightened the strap of his binoculars and rode away.

Amber sat on the couch, arms crossed over her chest. "I feel so *violated*."

"Don't worry about it," I cooed. I crouched in front of her, twining my fingers in hers and pressing her left wrist against the leather. My other hand traced the fine line of her collarbone.

"Don't." She pushed back.

"Relax," I said. "You're with me."

She struggled and I struggled back, as if she were some

younger kid giving me crap on the playground. I used my legs as leverage. She gripped my hands hard at the knuckles. Red-faced, sweating, she threw me off.

"Get out," she said through gritted teeth.

I left her house, my penis stiff and painful against my bicycle seat. As I rounded the corner of Craydon, I saw Trevor outside the Mail Bag, drinking a Slice. There was no hockey that afternoon. The Ullman boys were gone, and Trevor ruled the street.

"Stay away from Amber, creep," I told him. He took a long sip of his Slice. "If you come around again, I'll beat your ass."

Trevor pointed a thumb at his house. "You want to see my town?"

I consider this, the bicycle between us. I could have beaten him up without further discussion, but Mrs. Waddell might have seen; so much for my improved reputation. Maybe in his basement I could do what I liked. Besides, I couldn't lie: I was curious about our town.

I dropped my bike by the dogwood tree and followed him inside.

His house was the same—ashy clutter, stuffed muskrats. His mother was in the kitchen, staring at the flystrip dangling from the ceiling.

"You're back," she said. I could hear the eagerness in her voice. She must have thought it sad her son had so few friends.

We went down the basement steps. His city spread across the concrete floor. He must have made a deal with his mother because he no longer had to hide it. Not that he could, even if he'd wanted to. It had grown too large to conceal.

The individual buildings were impressive enough; each had tripled in size, without the model losing any of its symmetry. I could imagine dolls living in their empty rooms. But it was the aerial view from the third step that amazed me. From there I could see the town square laid out like a map, precise in its geometry, but with much more detail than a map could ever hope to accomplish: every hallway, every room, every window. The only thing wrong was the hodge-podge of color: gray walls spoiled by red and yellow blocks. He had to make do with inferior materials.

I leaned back and saw Elverton from a peaceful distance, huddled and serene. Then I leaned forward, peering through the rooms where no one lived—little cells that time passed through. How had he accomplished such detail when no one ever let him inside?

"Go ahead," Trevor said. "Walk around."

The shelving was gone from the walls, and there was a small perimeter around the town for visitors to move through. I walked around, glancing into windows. My own house was perfect, but I knew that already. I circled the square, looking for the house where Amber lived. Trevor had it exact, a white farmhouse gone to seed, the porch held up with diagonal beams to keep it stable. But it wasn't the outside that made me stop and stare; it was the way he'd built the details of the interior: the cut-out wall that linked Amber's living room and kitchen; the rickety stairs in the main hall that led up to her bedroom; even the bedroom itself, although I couldn't say for sure whether that room was accurate. I had no intimate knowledge.

I had a strange feeling, watching the model from above, like I was outside time and space, examining a memorial for something that hadn't yet been destroyed.

"What do you think?"

I imagined Trevor with binoculars, standing on the far edge of the road in the dark, training his eyes on Amber's bedroom. "You're sick."

Trevor chuckled. Maybe this was the response he'd hoped for—the viewer squirming in the palm of his hand. I thought about hitting him but didn't. I was in his world now. Some kind of curse might fall on me.

"I'm going home," I said.

"Fine," Trevor said. "I've got work to do."

I walked back out into the thick heat of late summer. I missed the sounds of the Ullman boys, their calls of C-A-R, the way they put the street in motion. The oldest one worked in a lumberyard now, and the second oldest had joined the army. They had few options, those violent boys. The rest of the gang spent their afternoons inside, watching television. Other than the buzzing of greenhead flies, Craydon Street was as silent as Trevor's model.

But inside our house, things were anything but quiet. My mother was home, but there was no dinner being prepared; instead, my father was winding himself up for the final speech, *Forward to the Future*. I remember the way he climbed up onto the table and the way it rocked beneath his feet. He spoke of the future as if it were a city you could go to, but only if you *worked hard* and were *vigilant*, because you couldn't well expect the future to simply *come to you*, it had to be continually *achieved, conquered, realized*—a perspective that frightened me at the time, punctuated by my father's vehement stomping and the clattering of cutlery, but that now strikes me as strangely optimistic. Conquering the future: what a dream!

Before he could finish, the table wobbled and broke beneath him, one leg splintering beneath his weight. He lost his balance on the sliding tabletop and fell face-first, hands and knees slamming against the linoleum. The twins shouted in excitement, my father moaned, and my mother got down on the floor, holding his head and telling him, *be still*.

"Idiots," my father muttered. "Ignorant savages."

"Quiet now," my mother said. "You need to rest."

My father stopped mumbling and started panting instead, a tired bull that had dragged us deep into the countryside and then collapsed.

I got up from my seat and went over to where the two of them were lying. I looked down at my helpless father, my foot pulled back as if to kick him. "Get up," I yelled. "You're the one who brought us here, you bastard."

But he didn't get up. My father panted, my mother whispered, and I looked out the window at the sleeping street, wondering if Trevor was outside, spying as my family fell apart.

I WENT TO REGIONAL THAT FALL. I was no lover anymore; Amber never spoke to me after Trevor came around with his binoculars. Rumor spread that he and I were in on it together, spying on naked girls in nighttime windows—and after my father became a patient at the Woodbury

Psychiatric Hospital, the neighborhood kids passed our house with suspicious glances, whispering and laughing.

I was no bully, either. Too many high school kids could kill me with a punch. I was just a gawky boy with clumsy legs and a temper, and I fell in with the kind of kids who fit in nowhere: skinny kids with long hair and bad acne, worn baseball caps and "Stairway to Heaven" bumper stickers. After school I would sit in the back of one of the older guys' pickups in the parking lot with a battery-powered radio blasting classic rock, and after we'd passed a covert jay, I'd lie with my back against the ridged bed and look up at the sky.

The weed pacified me. While the rest of the guys compared the asses of girls they'd never have the courage to speak to, I made a map out of clouds: Asia, Europe, the long tip of Patagonia. I thought that maybe I would join the Navy once I graduated—the branch of the military that had the least to do with direct killing. The Navy would take me away.

I sometimes saw Trevor during lunch, sitting on the other side of the massive cafeteria, surrounded by boys who played games with cards and dice. He hadn't grown much. Except for a faint mustache, he could still have passed for twelve.

How had I ever let such a tiny creature frighten me? He looked lonely, even surrounded by people. His eyes scanned the room like a dog let loose in an unfamiliar house.

One morning during my senior year, an announcement came over the loudspeaker while I was in shop. The teacher had us stop our saws and hammers and lathes; we stood and listened in the silence of the big machines.

Everyone report to the gym for an emergency address.

The entire student body crowded the gym, standing shoulder to shoulder—no time to assemble chairs—while the principal gave a speech.

"There has been a terrible accident in New York City," he murmured into the microphone—this short man with a comb-over, his voice thin even at the best of times. "You should all go home and be with your families."

Due to some obscure emergency procedure, we all had to wait for our parents to pick us up from school that day, and my mother was late. Once the rest of the students had filtered out through the main doors of the auditorium, confused in their parents' arms, my homeroom teacher took pity on me and walked me to the A/V room.

There were only ten or so students there, the television trained to a news program, the video loop of planes crashing, over and over. Trevor was there too, sitting in the front row. I didn't know anyone else in the room, so I sat down next to him.

Trevor turned to look at me. I could tell from his expression that he was afraid, and that seeing me in the seat next to him was a comfort. I was surprised to see Trevor frightened. I'd heard his father had died the year before—fallen drunk off the observation tower at Oyster Point—but I hadn't sought him out to offer sympathy. Maybe I'd been wrong all these years, ignoring him, insulting him, kicking him in the ribs. Maybe he had feelings after all.

Trevor leaned in and whispered. "Promise me that if something happens to me, you'll look out for the town," he said, as if no time had passed since we last spoke about his tiny city.

"I'll try," I said.

Was he manipulating me, the same way he'd manipulated me to get access to my house, back when I was young and vulnerable? I told myself it didn't matter. Here was my chance to redeem myself and show some kindness.

He grabbed my arm, hard. "Promise, Eddie. You're the only one I can trust."

"I promise."

"I still have so much work to do," he whispered.

My mother arrived to take me home, hurrying me on with a hand against my back. She always moved blindly forward, as if through constant motion you could outrun the fate that was gaining on you. "Hurry up," she whispered. "The twins are waiting in the car."

There was no time to consider what Trevor had told me. What did he mean, he had more work to do? How much could his little city grow, trapped in the basement? I'd promised to be the steward of something I didn't fully understand.

AFTER THE NATIONAL TRAGEDY, my mother decided to run. By this time, my father was out of Woodbury, living with his mother in the northern part of the state. We were told we'd have a chance to visit, once he was feel-

ing like himself again—but by then I'd more or less forgotten what that meant. There was nothing tethering us to
Elverton anymore. That March she made plans to sell our
house on Craydon Street and move to Pennsylvania. She'd
had enough.

"Why now?" I asked her, by which I meant: *Why not
before?*

"The twins'll be going to high school in September,"
she told me. "It'll be natural. If they stay here, they'll be
feral by Christmas."

"Who cares about the twins?" I asked, by which I
meant: *Who cares about me?*

I went to the school recruiter in the spirit of revenge.
Now that I was eighteen, I didn't need my mother's per-
mission. I asked him what I needed to join the Navy, and
he helped me fill out all the paperwork. The country was
going to war; there was a need.

When I told my mother about my decision—in late May,
just before my graduation—she put her face in her hands
and wept. The twins were in the living room, watching
television and throwing things at the walls. They were the
same age as I'd been when we moved to Elverton. What a
force of nature they'd become! They tore up shrubs and
flowers and dented the side of our family's shed with baseball bats.

"You too, Eddie?" she asked. "But you're the good one."

In the other room the twins were shouting at a cop
show: *kill him, kill him, kill him.* My poor mother's face
was stripped of pride. She'd taken up smoking to relieve

her stress, and she had fine lines everywhere. This town had dragged her down.

MY MOTHER SOLD THE PLACE QUICKLY; our move-out date was the end of June. I was expected to report for duty the first of July, but I had time to help her clean out the house. For days we labored, clearing out our history. My mother had sold whatever she could spare, but certain things remained: silverware, paintings, beautiful earthenware lamps—a few things kept clean and whole.

By the fourth day, the place was husked. Craydon Street was quieter than ever; all the Ullman boys were grown and had moved away. The nuclear plant was closing down, a casualty of failed inspections. Yet when I went outside to sneak a smoke, I saw that the world was dappled with light, the lawn a riot of magnolia bloom, those full and rotting flowers. The air held the seminal smell of dogwood, and the clovered grass of Trevor's lawn bristled with green. I knew he was down there, under the earth, fixing us all into position.

My mother joined me. "When's your bus?" she asked. "The twins want to go to Watertown for Chinese."

"Eight," I said. "But I have some business to take care of first."

My mother nodded, wiping her dusty hands on her jeans. We were long past expecting justification for each other's behavior.

I crossed Craydon Street and knocked on Trevor's door.

No one answered. I tried the handle, and the door swung open. I hesitated at the threshold, but only for a second. This was my last chance. Even if Trevor wasn't home, I was going to see what I'd come to see.

I don't know how Trevor and his mother lived in that empty place. I can only assume they'd sold most of their possessions, whether out of financial pressure or to pay for Trevor's materials. The coffee table, the piano, even the twin muskrats that used to fight on top of it, were all gone, and in their place, Trevor's magnificent city.

It was all aboveground now. Most of the houses were as tall as my knee, and some of the larger ones—the school, the fire department engine house—went all the way up to my waist. Each one was built from thousands of tiny bricks pressed together, the thin seams between them invisible to the naked eye. He had copied every windowsill, every balustrade, every piece of cracked and crippled molding, and instead of worrying over the colors of the blocks, he'd simply painted them, like any house, each shade a perfect copy of the source material. He'd even chipped the paint in places and faded it in others, mimicking the sun.

The model didn't depict the town as it was now, of course, but as it was at a single moment in the past, when we were thirteen: Market, Bacon's, Craydon, Ridgeway. A snapshot of the year 1997—a fall afternoon, soundless and still.

Trevor appeared in the dining room doorway. His thin mustache didn't make him look any older. He spoke as if he'd been telling the same story, with brief interruptions, for as long as we'd known each other.

"What do you think? I'm almost finished."

"My mom's moving away," I said.

He didn't seem to have heard me. He gestured to the town. "Do you like it? It's close, you know. Very close."

"Where's your mom, Trevor?" I asked. "Where do you *eat*?"

"She's *sick*," he spat. "I have to take care of her. I barely have any time to build. If it wasn't for *her*, I'd have been done a long time ago." He motioned to the tiny Craydon Street that split the carpet. "Go ahead. Take a walk."

I walked the path I had once taken with my fingers, counting off the buildings—*one, two, three*—until I got to *eleven* and saw it on the right, my empty house. The kitchen where my father fell from the table and babbled "savages"; the living room where the twins threw sticks at the television; the tiny bedroom where I once pulled on my penis in trembling silence—all the rooms stripped bare.

I'd barely been able to keep myself under control for four days, shuttling boxes. *This doesn't matter,* I'd told myself. *The minute you're out of here it'll begin to fade. Years will go by, and you won't think about it more than once or twice. Just a few years of your life. Just your childhood. Just the place you come from.*

I thought about breaking open the dollhouse with my foot, but instead I started crying.

There it was, all that evidence: my life, without me in it.

Trevor watched me silently until I finished crying. "But what do you *think*, Eddie?" he asked, urgently. "You're the only one who can tell me if it's perfect."

My eyes were red and raw. "Good-bye, Trevor," I said, and walked out the door.

IT'S BEEN FIVE YEARS since I've been back to Elverton. I live with the gray ocean, the choked whine of engines as planes take the tarmac and idle in their own smoke, the prison-quality meat they squeeze from a tube. A life of compression, its meaning squeezed into acronyms: DSG, LPOD, OOD.

The one good thing is the constant motion. It takes hundreds of men, moving in tandem, just to drive this metal carrier *forward*. Nobody turns his eyes to the wake. So when they asked me to go see my father, my mother, my brothers, I could say: my country needs me. I could face forward, toward the future.

Until this week, when I was back on leave, spending my Friday watching Animal Planet in my half-furnished apartment in Tacoma, and I got a call from a man with an official-sounding voice.

He asked if my name was Edward Monroe, as if it were written on a card.

I said it was.

Now this is going to sound odd, he said.

It was a lawyer, put in charge of the personal effects of one Trevor Harrison, and I can't say I was completely surprised by what he had to say—that Trevor had hung himself in the kitchen of his house, his mother long dead; that he'd buried her body himself and used her social security checks to buy more materials for building. The last, at least, was a surprise, although I'd always known he'd spare no expense for his masterpiece.

"Why are you telling me all this?" I asked, making my voice hard. "What does it have to do with me?" The man was clearly out of his element. "He wanted you to have that . . ." The man hesitated over the word. "That thing he built. He was very specific."

I said I'd be down on Monday.

It's Monday now.

I thought at first I'd make my mother do it. She still lives in Pennsylvania, so she's closer, and anyway the whole thing was more her fault than mine, how our family was wrecked on the rocks of that little town.

But no. Trevor is my responsibility. I made a promise.

I think I know what to do. I'll make the trip tonight, once the sun sets. I'll cross the bay on the bridge past Wilmington, get some gasoline at the Sunoco station near Watertown, and then I'll rocket through the marshland, windows down, smelling the rotting gingko berries. I'll park a-ways from Trevor's, so no one will see my car.

I don't know what I'll find when I open up that dusty house. Maybe the town will have grown still higher, buildings tall as my chest, straining against the walls, houses inside houses. It doesn't matter. The only question is how to put an end to it. I could pour gasoline across the floor, trailing a little bit through the screen door, and drop a match—if not for the neighbors. Who knows? I'm sure the story of Trevor has gotten out by now, and maybe they're as frightened of that tiny city as I am.

But most likely I'll do what I've always done and use my hands, though it's hard to imagine myself standing over our town like a movie monster, ripping it apart. Maybe this was always Trevor's plan for me, his dare. He was right, I'm no builder—but I can break things down.

BAR JOKE, ARIZONA
\\\\\\\\

A MAN WALKS INTO A BAR. He walks over to the bartender and says, "Can I get a drink?"

The bartender looks up from the fan he's been tinkering with and says, "Sure. What would you like?"

"Well," the man says, "the problem is, I don't have any money."

"I see," the bartender says. It's a stifling day, the bar has no air conditioning, and with the fan broken, the heat's starting to bother him.

"But I do have . . ."

The man starts, then breaks off, hesitates, and begins again.

145

"I have . . . oh . . . wait . . . hold on."

The bartender shakes his head and starts washing some glasses.

"Look, I have—you know," the man mumbles, gesturing in the air. "Oh, I used to remember this one. Gimme a second."

Finally he gives up and stares at his hands.

The bartender finishes washing the glasses, throws the rag over his shoulder, and gives the man a hard look.

"You forgot the punch line, didn't you?" the bartender asks.

The man looks down at the bar and nods sadly.

"It happens," the bartender says. "You have good days, and then you have bad days."

"What do we do now?" the man asks. "Where do we go from here?"

The man looks he might start to cry, which makes the bartender feel a little queasy.

"All right, boyo," the bartender says. "C'mon now. Buck up." He checks the door. The barflies are all at home, sleeping through the heat. Nobody ever comes to the bar this early on a Saturday.

"Look," he says, "let's start this whole thing over."

"Really?" the man says, perking up.

"Sure. But on one condition. You get behind the bar."

The man shakes his head violently.

"I don't have any bartending experience," he says. "I wouldn't know the first thing about it."

"It's easy," the bartender says. "I've been doing it for years. Your part's all logical."

"I'm not too good with logic," the man says.

"Do me a favor," the bartender says. "It'd be nice for me to get out from behind here for a few minutes. It'd do me good."

The man takes a deep breath and rubs his temples with the tips of his fingers.

"All right," the man says. "I'll give it a try."

The bartender smiles and wipes his hands on the rag. Without taking their eyes off of each other, the man and the bartender circle the bar and exchange places. All of a sudden, the broken fan rumbles and begins to whir.

"Go ahead," the man says. "I think I'm ready."

"Can I get a drink?" the bartender asks.

"Sure," the man says. "What would you like?"

"Well," the bartender says, "I have to tell you, I'm flat broke. I don't have a red cent to my name. There's nothing but lint in my pockets."

"In that case," the man says, pulling a beer out of the cooler, "this one's on the house."

He slides the beer across the counter. The bartender just stares at it. "Hey, look," he growls, pointing his finger at the man's chest. "What are you trying to pull? We had a real simple deal here. You're the straight man. It's all logical. A monkey could do it."

"I know, I know," the man says. "But let me tell you something: it's nice back here. Look at all these bottles of liquor, lined up by type. It's really something."

The bartender looks at the bottles, amber and light brown, white frosted glass.

"They're all right," he admits.

"Do yourself a favor," the man says, putting his hands out, palms up. "Drink your beer. Relax. Take a breath. Didn't you say yourself that you needed a break?"

The bartender considers this. "I'm more tired than I've been in my entire life," he says. "It seems like it's the same bit every time, over and over."

"That's because it is," the man says.

The bartender doesn't respond. He takes a sip of his beer.

AFTER A MINUTE, the door swings open, and a duck waddles into the bar.

"Hey," the duck says, hopping onto a barstool. "Got any duck food?"

"Look," the man says, "I'm new here, and I know this might seem strange, but how about we just cut the whole routine and I give you a drink? On the house. Because we're all a little tired here today, and we're not in the mood for gags."

The duck turns his beady eyes toward the man, then the bartender, and then the man again. He flaps his wings, shakes his ass, and hunkers down on the barstool.

"Jesus Christ," the duck says. "I sure could use one."

"What are you having?" the man says, smiling.

"Give me a Wild Turkey, straight up," the duck says. "For starters."

"How's the week coming, Duck?" the bartender asks.

"Just fucking dandy," the duck says. "Thanks for fucking asking."

Before long, a man with a large hat walks through the door. He moseys up to the bar, takes off his hat, and sets it on the table.

"Let me guess," the man says. "You've got a little guy inside that hat."

The man with the hat blushes. "Is it that obvious?" he asks.

"It's just one of those things," the man replies. "Does he want a drink?"

"Are you kidding me?" a muffled voice shouts from inside the hat. "I'd love one!"

Soon the place starts filling up with men: guys with speech impediments, guys with eye patches, sailors with wooden legs talking to tax attorneys. The animals arrive, too. People keep tripping over a boa constrictor and cursing. In one corner a bear and a sperm whale are communicating through grunts and clicks.

"Don't tell the management," the bartender whispers to the man. "We haven't made any money all day."

"But look how happy everyone is," the man says. "It's a beautiful thing."

"It won't change anything," says the bartender. "Just you wait."

As if to prove this point, a man bursts through the door and runs full-tilt toward the bar, his head hung low like a bull charging the cape. A priest, a minister, and a rabbi all grab onto his coat to restrain him, but even with their collective strength they can barely keep him from slamming his head into the wood.

"What are you people doing?" the bar rusher yells. "Let

a man do his goddamn job! Let a man DO HIS MOTHER-FUCKING JOB ALREADY!" And since he can't make physical contact with the bar itself, he starts to shout "Ouch! Ouch!" over and over again.

"Be still, my son," the priest says, wiping his forehead with a damp rag. "Be still. You have seen the trials of this life, but you will be forgiven in the life to come."

"Have some bourbon," says the minister, handing him a glass. "There's no law against it, on heaven or earth."

"If you ask me," says the rabbi, "the boy needs therapy."

The three holy men lean over the bar rusher and whisper comforting words. The other customers begin to take notice and turn toward the scene. Some make the sign of the cross; others murmur prayers.

"I'm sorry," the bar rusher says, sipping his whiskey. "I'm so sorry. I'm a basket case; I can't relax. My hair's starting to fall out, and I can't sleep. My wife left me for a man who writes ad copy. A more advanced animal altogether. How can anyone keep up these days?"

The whole bar nods in agreement.

"Let me ask your opinion," the bar rusher says to the three holy men. "I know God's view on the meek and the lowly, but what about the middling kind of shit-kicker? What about the overgrown suburban lawn with the unpruned rosebushes, the ungrateful kids, and the low-paying 401(k)? I need to know: does God smile on mediocrity?"

"Of course," says the priest.

"Maybe," says the minister.

"No," says the rabbi.

The bar rusher lays his head in the priest's lap and starts to weep.

"I feel for you," says the man with the hat. His little man is drunk, passed out on the table and snoring. "My dad was a bricklayer who hung out at the Polish Society Hall. Now people talk to each other on computers, no one knows how to fix an engine, and I've got dyspepsia like you wouldn't believe. I take pills upon pills, and it never gets any better. It's a beat-up dog of a world."

Night falls. It's a perfect example of a Southwestern American sky, clear and nullifying all humanity. The stars are like pinpricks in a cloth that keeps everybody ignorant of what's really going on. Everyone fumbles around by the light of a sickle-cell moon.

Under cover of darkness the conversations get lower and less animated. Stories emerge from the chatter. Eyes grow damp, and the alcohol pulls secrets and failures out of everybody's wobbly mouths.

"I remember I was lying in bed once," a giant moth says, his diaphanous wings glowing in the light of the hanging lamp. "With my wife. 'You're a one-trick pony,' she told me. 'It's always a cycle with you, one joke over and over again, a bad ride that never ends.'"

The moth has a small, buzzing voice, like someone over a bad long-distance connection saying words nobody wants to hear. It shakes a little from too much crème de menthe.

"All I could think of," the moth says, "was her spinning slowly in a Ferris wheel in the middle of an empty county fair, stuck in a seat with a guy like me, who didn't have much to say. That was the night she left me for a man who sells funny T-shirts over the Internet. They can travel whenever they want, she tells me. They're globe-trotters now."

The moth's wings fall to his sides, and his wide gray feelers wave in the dim light. His drunken friends, two large fruit flies, are drinking sweet liquor through straws. They rub their legs together in a penitent fashion and buzz mournfully.

The clock edges toward closing time. Most of the customers have already fallen asleep in their beer. The sperm whale has himself beached against the far wall, and three bears are sleeping in his shadow, wrapped in each other's arms. The bar rusher sleeps with his head on the priest's shoulder, face pressed against the cool cloth of his vestments. Half-asleep himself, the priest strokes the bar rusher's soft, thinning hair. The minister and the rabbi sleep with their faces turned to the heavens.

By the time the duck hops onto an empty table in the middle of the bar, the only sound is the wheezy pull of the whole bar breathing, strained and rough, like a giant set of smoker's lungs or a broken accordion. He gives a couple of loud honks. Shocked out of sleep, everyone pricks up his ears.

"Friends," the mallard says, flapping his wings. "I'd like to tell you a story. It's not a funny one, but it's something I've been wanting to tell for a long time, and I've never really known how to do it. So I thought I'd tell you all tonight, since you're all now my friends, and it's been a pleasure knowing each and every one of you, you've really made a duck feel welcome. That's a rare thing in this cold world."

Little calls of joy and affirmation flare up around the room. The duck waits for them to die down before going on.

"When I was a younger duck," he says, "I lived in a large city on the eastern side of this fair nation. It was a hell of a fucking town, let me tell you. There were lights on all twenty-four hours of the day and places you could crawl into at four o'clock in the morning where someone would buy you a drink and scratch your tail feathers for you, if that was what you were in the mood for. Paradise on earth.

"And of course, I had a girl I was with, a beautiful fox who lived in a second floor walk-up, right over a club where they played jazz on Wednesdays and Saturdays. Now, in those days and even now, a relationship between a fox and a duck wasn't very common, and there were only a few places we could go and not get looks, even threats. The club she lived above was one of them. We spent a lot of nights there before going up to her room. The Wednesday band was good; the Saturday band was better. They had a trumpet player who made big gorilla men weep tears for love.

"But you get tired of the same old thing, y'know? So one day my fox, she says to me, 'Let's go to the symphony. I've never seen the symphony. I think a fox ought to have seen the symphony at least once in her life.'

"Now, I'm strictly a whiskey and beer sort of bird, not what anyone would call 'sophisticated.' But I thought,

Hell, why not, the lady wants a bit of culture, I might as well accompany her on this particular social engagement. We got dressed up on a Friday night and went off to the symphony.

"The hall was a big place with gold leaf all over. It was a real class joint, and I didn't feel like we fit in, but we found our seats and waited for the show to begin. All those people in black ties had their instruments ready. Have any of you ever heard an orchestra tune up? I bet you probably haven't."

Nobody makes a sound. The duck sighs and examines his wings.

"I didn't think so. The orchestra," he continues, "was all right. I don't really remember what they played. I remember I liked it at first, but as it went on I had a hard time staying awake. It wasn't that I didn't like it, but it made me sleepy. My fox didn't much like it. She liked dressing up, she liked the pomp and circumstance, but the music left her cold.

"So you could ask me why I remember. Why I'm bringing it up. A fair question. Because although the music wasn't really all that thrilling, there was this one thing that stuck with me. After the musicians had tuned, after the conductor came out and there was a big round of applause for him, after the musicians had all settled into their seats, that was when the whole hall filled with a moment of absolute, wonderful silence. Quiet like you wouldn't believe. Bows raised, lips on mouthpieces, and of course my fox in the seat next to me, her heart hammering, like it always did whenever she was waiting for something she thought might be exciting. A whole room waiting, desperately quiet.

"After the show, we went back to her apartment. We were tired, and we went to bed without touching each other much. I listened to the traffic noise in the night like I always did when I was trying to go to sleep, but for the first time it didn't seem soothing. It just made me wish for a kind of silence that wasn't there in the twenty-four-hour city."

The duck gets quiet for a second. Outside some drunk is singing a tuneless song. It makes the duck wince. The drunk passes on, and the song dies away.

"There isn't really a good end to the story," the duck says, in a softer voice. "Suffice to say, the thing with the fox and me didn't work out. I started wandering all over the city at night; it was spring and I was restless. I went to the symphony a few times by myself, but in that silence I was telling you about I felt so lonely I couldn't even stand it. So I stopped going.

"I moved out here to the desert to try to get away from her. It's quieter here. I stopped talking to people. I even made a pilgrimage out into the desert once, with a bunch of Buddhist mystics who wanted to live totally mute. They never said a word to each other the whole time we were out there.

"But despite my best intentions, I could never do it. I would walk over to a cliff and sit and watch the sky, and I'd feel that itching in my throat. It started at the back, close to my spine, and worked its way upward. My beak twitched. I started muttering, mumbling. And then it would start. I'd start talking to the canyon.

" 'How's the weather?' I'd ask. 'How's your parents? A man walks into a bar. Let me tell you about my new car. Are you married? I love you. I miss you. What's your sign? Where were you born? I'm lonely. Do you have any duck food?'

"Just me talking to the canyon," the duck says, his beak trembling. "And then I'd get up and go back to the Buddhists. They'd nod at me. I'm pretty sure they knew what I was doing, but they never let on.

"Someday," the duck says. "Someday I'm going to shut up, and it'll be the happiest day of my life."

The duck gets quiet. He shakes his tail feathers, lays down on the table, and closes his eyes.

Men are sleeping again, slumped in chairs or spread across the dirty floor. Nobody speaks, except for the occasional whisper coming out of someone's lonesome dream. The man and the bartender consider one another. The clock reads 2:15. Outside people are stumbling across the road, falling into one another, stumbling all over the place.

"We ought to kick them out soon," the bartender says. "You can't let people stay all night."

"Show some kindness," the man says. He starts wiping the bar in long, slow strokes, shaking his head softly. "Show a little kindness for once in your life."

THE GREAT AMERICAN SONGBOOK
\\\\\\\\

> *"The effect of music is so very much more powerful and*
> *penetrating than is that of the other arts, for these others*
> *speak only of the shadow, but music of the essence."*
> —SCHOPENHAUER, *THE WORLD AS WILL*
> *AND REPRESENTATION*

1. To a Broadway Rose
(for Lana Turner)

You smiled for the cameras, Lana, while the band played
"To a Broadway Rose." You danced like the choreogra-
pher told you to dance, only you stumbled. You were nervous up there in your stage clothes: white blouse and bow

157

tie, tap shoes shined. Only nineteen years old—no wonder you were nervous. Who could blame you for having a drink or two in your dressing room to calm your nerves? Only sometimes you were so nervous that you had more than two, more than four, and when the cameras started rolling, you were too drunk to do whatever it was you were nervous about, a fact which only made you more nervous, so that with the drinking and the nervousness you were totally incapable of doing the dance—"To a Broadway Rose."

That morning you didn't want me to leave the bed. You held onto my leg like a little girl, *Five more minutes, Artie, just five more minutes*, and when the two of us split up at the soundstage door, you looked so much like a kid that I felt guilty letting you loose among the wolves. An older husband is supposed to be protective.

"Trust me, Artie," you said. "I know what I'm doing."

I said the same thing at nineteen.

"Take five," the director called. "Ready, Mr. Shaw?"

"Born ready," I said.

The camera magazines started spinning, and you took your place, the only sign of weakness a quiver in the side of your mouth. I loved that quiver, Lana. You had that quiver the first time I laid a hand on you at Maxine's in Pasadena and plucked you from the crowd. You thought you were only a minor character, but I knew better. I wasn't the only one watching you from the bandstand.

"Cut." That fat man's voice through the megaphone—"For the love of God, cut."

"One more," I told the band. "Just one more."

They grumbled. This was hackwork: playing dance music for the boss's drunken wife.

"I'm ready, Mr. Simon," you said. You made the quiver in your mouth stop.

I took the first solo. I took it over and over.

Set up. Action. Take eight. We had a gig to play that night at the Hotel Pennsylvania, and the boys' stomachs were groaning. They hated that song by the end of the day, "To a Broadway Rose," lips all swollen and the rhythm burned into their brains. When they went to bed that night after the incident at the Rose Room, they barely noticed their wives and girlfriends and children and dogs, because the song was dancing its way around their skulls.

You were sweating so much under the hot, white lights that the makeup woman had to come pat you off between takes, but still you stared those cameras down like a drunk stares down a cop and said, *I'm ready now.*

Anybody could see you weren't ready. You wouldn't be ready until someone put seven cups of coffee and maybe some Benzedrine in your system. You were too young for the picture—you wouldn't be ready for your close-up for another few years—but the camera was trying to make up the difference by wearing you down. Every time the director hollered *cut* and the slate slapped down, your face got harder. Every take aged you a little, brought you closer to maturity. Your eyes narrowed, you pursed your lips and sneered. Then the magazine started whirring, and you came to life again, a smile plastered across your face.

Take eighteen, take nineteen. I couldn't maintain. I yelled at the director, trying to smile like it was a joke: "Sylvan, hey, Sylvan, do you think we could do a different number just for variety's sake because it's killing the boys, let me tell you, playing this same number a hundred times, and it's got to be killing Lana too, having to listen to it."

I was only trying to be kind, Lana. I'm not very good, but I tried, even though you turned to me like I had just insulted your mother's sexual hygiene and said "It doesn't matter what song you play, Artie; they dub it anyway. Every song's the same. Every band in America could play that song. A trained monkey could play that song. Nobody cares what you think, Mr. Shaw, you dumb Hebe. You don't know a damn thing about the movie business. Why don't you and your boys blow another dumb tune, and let the rest of us get on with the picture?"

I held the clarinet like I might snap it in half. I would have come down and cocked you across the face, but I was trapped in the frame with the band laughing behind me.

"Set up," the director called. "Take twenty."

I put the horn back to my lips and blew the melody as hard as I could while you came toward me across the stage, heavy makeup holding your smile in place. You could have been any age under that smile: nineteen, twenty-seven, thirty-five. You were locked in. Your heels kept time with the cymbal and the clarinet as your black skirt flipped up at all the right moments, and when you ended the dance with a perfect spin and the number was over, the band took their horns from their lips and the whole studio paused for a moment of silence, the director's wet cigar dropping into his lap, as you turned to me and said, "Don't you ever tell me anything about my business, Artie, because I am a professional."

They asked me plenty of questions after I walked off-stage at the Rose Room. The papers wanted to know why the world's most famous clarinetist would give up a musical career worth several million dollars and a Hollywood wife for a cabin in the middle of Pennsylvania and nothing but a typewriter and the collected works of Schopenhauer to keep him company. I could have said: *Hatred is an affair of the heart; contempt is an affair of the head*. I could have said it was because of the fat man with his cup full of spit-chewed tobacco screaming at my wife. I could have said it was because I went to bed that night alone in the spare bedroom while you broke plates in the pantry and the idiot melody of "To a Broadway Rose" echoed in my brain.

But the truth is, Lana, you were right. You are a professional, and I am something else.

2. My Blue Heaven
(to Carter Blondestone)

You watched that man stab a pen into my leg, Carter. He walked up to the bandstand at the Rose Room in the Hotel Pennsylvania and rammed it into my thigh. Maybe he didn't mean it. Maybe he just meant to tap me and get my attention. Maybe he was half-insane from two hours of jitterbugging, dizzy and dehydrated and generally not thinking clearly. He was past the point of restraint. We all were.

"Fucking hell," I said.

When I looked down, I saw him looking up at me with crazy eyes, holding out the pen in one hand and a napkin in the other. The tip of the pen was all bloody. At first I thought he was offering me the napkin to clean up the blood, but then I realized he didn't notice the blood at all. What he wanted was for me to sign my name on the napkin.

"Fucking hell," I said.

I don't think he noticed me talking. Maybe he was drunk, maybe hopped up, maybe just hysterical. Everybody in the crowd was hysterical. You couldn't hear what anyone said over the screaming. You couldn't even hear the notes coming out of your own horn. That was how I learned how to read lips. I could read this guy's lips, easy. I could see them mouthing *autograph*.

"Fucking hell," I said. I kicked him in the face.

That was when you ran up, Carter, to save me from myself. You picked up the man and brushed him off, and while he was dazed, you took the pen away from him and put it in your pocket. I guess you would say you did it for my own protection, but I know better.

My leg throbbed like hell where the pen had gone in, and I figured I would probably need a doctor before the night was over. I couldn't hear myself think over the screaming, much less play the horn, and I took the clarinet from my lips and swung it down onto the stage like it was a baseball bat, watching it break into pieces. The crowd screamed for more. I remember you dropped that man to the floor and stared at the broken instrument in my hands. I bet *mistake* was the first word that entered your head. You loved that clarinet. From the minute you looked into the black bell at the end of it, you recognized a highly sophisticated moneymaking machine. You didn't understand the human cost. You didn't understand the damage those songs did to my brain, night after night, those four-note melodies and stale changes. No wonder I can't think straight anymore, my head all full of songs.

What were you going to do with that pen, Carter? What were you doing with yourself all those years while I played eight sets a day at the Marlborough, one hour apiece, blowing solo after solo? What were you doing while girls clawed at my shoes and boys too young to drink pulled at my pant leg and screamed for autographs until the ambulances came and carried them out on stretchers? You were busy counting coins. You even shook down the officers of the goddamn Official Artie Shaw fan club for the membership fee they collected from those teenage suckers with bad skin: *twenty-five cents to join*. You weren't going to let a pen soaked in the blood of Artie Shaw slip away.

What did you do with that pen, Carter? Did you auction it off like a relic to the Fan Club? I hear you want me declared incompetent or loony or whatever the judge needs to declare me to put my money up for grabs. I bet you'll sign the papers with the same pen the crazy man stuck into my thigh. If you haven't sold it yet.

It's cold in this cabin, but I don't let it bother me. The stove draws nice. I'm working hard on my novelistic philosophical treatise on Schopenhauer, music, and the nature of mankind. It won't make me a dime. It won't make you a dime either, in case you were wondering. *Life is a business that does not cover the costs.*

You wouldn't understand, Carter. Every day the sun rises and turns the snow as blue as the sky. Every day I write a little more. I figure I'll finish it come Christmas, and when I come back to the city, I will carry it in triumph over my head like a brick to smash your sophisticated adding machine to pieces.

3. Everything is Jumpin'
(to Buddy Bechet)

There are good days and there are bad days, Buddy. You used to say that all the time. Back then I thought you were dumb, but now I know the truth of it.

There are good days when the snow melts a little and the typewriter keeps good time. There are bad days when I throw myself naked into the snow.

There are good days when the storekeeper Sven takes my money and hands me my beans without asking questions, when Alma of Alma's Restaurant brings the bacon without inquiring about my line of work. There are days when the snow is soft and I can walk for hours through the forest listening to the sound of my own voice.

There are bad days when a badger pisses in the woodpile.

There are good days when I think of you, Buddy, and the way we traded fours at the Adelaide after hours. I'm sorry I spat on you at Sinclair's, I'm sorry I fined you twenty bucks for missing a cue at the Royal, I'm sorry about Dorothy and the torn dress and the grease spot. I paid you nothing but peanuts. I treated you like a field hand, and you never complained when I was up in a penthouse with Lana eating caviar and lighting my cigars with dollar bills. You are just lousy with fundamental human decency.

"Call the tune, Buddy," I used to say.

You smiled. "Don't matter to me," you said. "I play anything. 'Sweet Georgia Brown,' maybe. Why not?"

"Jesus, Buddy," I said. "'Sweet Georgia Brown'? Do me a favor. Call something sophisticated."

"Whatever you want, boss," you said. "All the same to me. I play anything. 'Stardust,' I guess."

"Jesus Christ," I said. "'Stardust'? Don't give me that cheese, Buddy. Give me something with a little grit, a little bounce."

I called the tune myself.

I used to try to make you listen to *real music*: Stravinsky, Strauss, and Mahler; Debussy and Schoenberg. Something complex, something with heft, something to keep the mind from rusting. In the words of the master: *The composer reveals the innermost nature of the world. He expresses the profoundest wisdom in a language that his reasoning faculty does not understand.*

I locked you into a studio at RCA and made you listen to Ravel on the hi-fi: the String Quartet in F Major.

"Nice," you said. "Real nice."

You picked up your horn and played the violin line. You picked it out by ear.

"Nice," you said. "I dig it."

You plucked the line out of the air and played it a few times, turning it around, chopping it and cutting it and pasting it back together. I turned off the hi-fi and listened to you play. You were a natural.

"Sounds a little like this," you said.

You played "Stardust."

To you there was no difference. To me it was the difference between standing by the sea with a beer in your hand and bashing your own face in with a ball-peen hammer.

You left, and I stayed behind. I tried to play the same line you did, but every time I missed it, and I had to start the record again. I tried for hours, but no matter how many times I tried, it always hung in the air, just out of my reach. Finally I threw over the phonograph. I took the record and broke it against the wall.

4. Any Old Time
(to Billie Holiday)

I remember you, Billie, sitting with your skirt hitched up on the side counter in Sal's Kitchen and humming some stupid love song to yourself between bites: "Any Old Time." I snuck an eye between your legs while you sang. You made that song sound sophisticated.

You caught me looking.

"See anything you like?" you asked.

"You're the only thing I like," I said.

You laughed. You turned your head away and kept on singing.

We were sitting in Sal's Kitchen after hours waiting for

the train to take me away to Pennsylvania while you sang to yourself in front of an empty plate: "Any Old Time." But that's not true—it's not any old time, it's one time and then it's over. I had to borrow money from you for the train ticket because the banks were closed and I didn't want to go home. I feel bad now, knowing I might never see you again.

"Shoe's on the other foot," you said, "Mr. Millionaire." You gave me the money anyway.

It's hard to get any thinking done out here, Billie. The cabin's cold. I spend most of my time keeping myself alive, cutting wood and keeping it out of the snow. I can hear animals moving outside, smelling out food. I can hear their claws clicking around the walls, and my head is always full of songs. I didn't bring my clarinet, but it sings anyway, inside my skull.

Do you remember when we stood backstage at the Forrest drinking and you said you thought music was a curse because sometimes you couldn't sleep at night with the numbers running through your head? You used to say you were stupid, but I know you know how smart you are. Everything I know now, you knew a long time ago.

Reason is feminine in nature; it can only give after it has received. Of itself it has nothing but the empty forms of its operation.

That one gets me every time.

I lie on the floor of the cabin and look up at the ceiling. I let my mind drift, but whatever empty space I find fills up with songs. I lie there like the way I first found you,

Billie, lying in the upper room of Sal's, tied off and sleepy. You were eighteen years old and far from home. You knew all about this before I ever did.

5. *Nightmare*
(to Sal Figgliero)

Send me some money, Sal. I need it to survive.

Send me some money so I can pay the surly little store-keeper named Sven who sells me my beans. Now that he knows I'm Artie Shaw, he expects serious money. He's jacking up the prices. He's running credit I can't pay. Carter's holding my income against breach of contract. Lana's lawyering me to death. I'm fighting for my survival here. I need to keep up my strength. I need to eat. I need to concentrate if I'm going to finish this book before it reaches up from the typewriter and chokes me with my own words.

Send me some money, Sal. I don't ask for much after all I did for you. Didn't I buy you a Rolls to make up for sleeping with your sister? Didn't I put your trombone front and center? You were working a dime an hour before I picked you out of the lineup. Now I'm down here in the snow and the shit trying to survive among wild animals, and you won't even answer a simple request for human decency. I should've given the money to Buddy. He's a member of the angel band. I should have given it to Billie to spend on China white. Instead I stuffed the pockets of a sinner who can't hold his liquor and who shuns his brother in time of need.

Pay me some money, Sal. Pay me so I can pay Alma at the restaurant. Pay me so she'll stop asking me to sit in with that shoestring band that plays on Wednesdays and comes untuned every second measure. So she'll stop assuring me that everything is on the house. So I can finally slip her a hundred-dollar bill and earn some silence.

In the words of the master: *The less one has to come into contact with people, the better off one is for it.*

Send me some money, Sal. I'm at the mercy of these vicious people. They know I'm on the ropes. They're scenting blood. They're moving through the woods like animals, searching for this cabin. They're waiting outside in the drifts to catch me by surprise. They'll bring their torches and camp outside of my window at midnight in their horrible peasant clothes like pogrom victims and demand I play the clarinet in exchange for beans and bacon. These savages. They'll use their yellow country teeth to tear me apart.

6. *Nocturne*
(to Mother)

You're dead, Momma, but I talk to you anyway.

You're dead, but I don't forgive you for it. Remember those days when you made me play in the living room, when you made me play my clarinet for the New Haven ladies you were always trying to impress? Those New Haven ladies didn't like Jewish women as a rule, did they, Momma, but you were always an optimist. You thought your bright little boy with his clarinet was going to impress them. I sat in the middle of the room while you served those little tasteless crackers with flat cheese for the Gentiles, I played poor versions of Schubert's "Serenade" like a trained parrot, sweating bullets in the overcranked steam heat under the beady eyes of the New Haven ladies who didn't like Jewish women, as a rule, or their Jewish sons, as a rule, but who were willing to make an exception for particular talent.

Everybody is always willing to make an exception for particular talent.

You were banking on your boy, weren't you, Momma? Making him play for an hour with his cheeks going red from the effort and the steam heat you provided for the New Haven ladies on account of their icy blood. You made your boy perform although he hated everything about it, even the clarinet itself, the woody taste of the reed and its girlish tone. Everything except the applause, of course. I've always loved applause.

You even made me play when the ladies didn't come, on those lonely nights when I sat in the kitchen and watched you cry over Papa, our personal deadbeat. You said, *Please Artie, please play a little for the neighbors.* You liked for me to open the window and play out into the night. You were proud of your boy, because by then I'd learned to swing a little, I didn't need music, I just improvised sheets of sound for the benefit of the passersby. All those people who spat at your feet as you limped to services on Saturday, all those kids who shoved my head into the locker and kicked my legs out from under me in the halls, all of them stood on their lawns in their sport coats and loosened ties and listened to me blow. I remember them swaying in the blue night while you wept over your man and your boy.

When I finished, the people didn't even clap. They just

stood there, staring, hungry for more. So I put that awful thing back to my lips and started all over again.

You're dead, Momma, but while I sit here alone in this cabin in the darkest part of morning, I feel like you're watching me from the trees. You want me to play a little just for you.

6. I Let a Song Go Out of My Heart
(to Betty Kern)

I've had enough, Betty—I'm coming back.

You told me to come home when I had enough, lying on the bed on Seventeenth Street in sweet self-satisfaction, as if you knew I'd have enough sooner or later, as if your body was the land and I was the ship, bound to return someday. I hated you for saying it then, and I hate you even more now that I'm saying it myself, but I've had enough.

We had a blizzard come through Friday. Yesterday afternoon when I put on skis it was already heavy on the ground, but I needed supplies, Betty. I had a knife in my stomach from hunger, and it was impossible to think. I went to Cordalia despite the weather. When I was done with my shopping, I went to Alma's for dinner to clear my head. I thought I could still go home on my skis. I didn't realize it was the kind of blizzard you could get lost in.

I've had enough of Cordalia, I thought, sitting there in Alma's restaurant chewing a pork chop and watching that shoestring band assembling themselves around a cheap wooden stage, thin wood planks and two-by-fours bolted to the wall. The clarinetist looked at me in fear, like I was going to take him to task for his tone, and maybe he was right to be afraid, considering that last week I threw my typewriter against the wall of the cabin and burned everything I'd written in the stove.

I've had enough of music, I thought, sitting in that disgusting little diner with checkered tablecloths and the crumbs of previous customers sitting greasy in the cracks where the tablecloths slipped, watching the guitarist tuning and the drummer scratching a big boil on his face, listening with disgust as they started playing a version of "Stardust" so slow and stupid it sounded like a record played at the wrong speed. The clarinetist looked at me like he wanted my approval as the crowd of stocky German townies walked the floor and held each other with their sad and drunken hands.

Then the band played "Flat Foot Floogie."

I've had enough of hackneyed vocals and stumbling swing, I've had enough of whiny cornet and barnyard trombones. I've had enough of marketplace jingles and licensing rights, I've had enough of dancing and singing and other people's happiness.

When they tried to play "Flat Foot Floogie," I did a bad thing, Betty. I went up to the bandstand and pulled the clarinet out of that poor idiot's hands. I took it, and I started to play.

I was rusty at first but not for long. I am the greatest clarinet player in the world.

I took over that song. I blew a hole through its boring chords, I blew until I thought a vein in my brain would pop, but my brain stayed strong; they finished "Flat Foot

Floogie," but I wouldn't let them end, I'd had enough of
endings. I made them segue into their next number, "Choo
Choo Cha Boogie," blowing sweet while they stumbled behind me; I played rough with "Smooth Sailing," I had a
tender time with "Pennies from Heaven," remembering
Billie, I scared the shit out of the audience blowing stac-
cato blasts over "Boogie Woogie Bugle Boy," I played for
a half hour, then an hour, and I could see the audience
standing shocked in front of me like I was holding a gun
at them and they didn't know what I wanted them to do.
Several men cried during "Beyond the Sea." I almost cried.
I never cry. Finally, in the middle of the final chorus of
"Cheek to Cheek," chipping away at my own melody one
note at a time until it was more silence than sound, I felt
my legs give way and I fell to the bandstand.

I had enough of playing. The café was quiet. Men re-
moved their hats.

"Well," said the man whose clarinet I stole. "You sure
know a lot of songs, Mr. Shaw."

I'd had enough of idiots, Betty. In this I include myself.

"Songs," I said. "You motherfucker, songs? You don't
know what a *song* is, not if you had it tattooed on your
tiny left ball, not if you stuck your hand into an electrical
socket attached to the biggest radio in the fucking world.
Songs? Your fucking *band* can play a song, your *clarinet*
can play a song, your fucking *mother* can play a song! A
song is a fucking coffin! It's your wife recording what you
say in your sleep, your cornet player cadging a dollar, your
mother making you dance for her *amusement*! Songs are
what the roughnecks hum while they cave your head in,

songs are what the taxi drivers play while they *run down orphans in the street*. Songs are for organ grinders who fuck their sleeping monkeys, songs are for the children they fucking *birth* together! Songs is about not *thinking*, songs is about *dancing* like a *caged bear*, songs is about your lips stuck in a fucking *iron door* and then they ask you to *sing a song*, my friend, *for our amusement*. Songs from when you're born until you die, songs for a quarter, songs for a fucking *dime,* songs for your mother, your father, your unfaithful wife: they love you, you lucky motherfucker, bless you and your stupid little worthless life and your endless, idiot, imbecilic, godforsaken, all-encompassing shitbrained good-for-nothing mind-killing abomination of a *song*. Don't you get it, motherfucker? *A song spits on your grave*."

I gave the man his clarinet back and walked out into the snow.

Think of nothing under that curtain of white. Head out into trackless country. Listen to trees breathing in the frozen air. Think about snow, uncaring snow, snow falling soundlessly across a great distance, the blindness of snow, snow unseen, the softness of snow, snow at peace, the coldness of snow, snow muffling the motion of trees, snow as static, cutting out the sound of a radio. Let the falling snow cover everything. Let the song go out of your heart, let it go. I sat down there in the drifts, listening to the sound of nothing at all, letting the emptiness fill my mind until all I could hear was the sound of nothing falling, the sound of no songs.

You know the story, Betty—it was in the papers. How

Artie Shaw went deranged, how he played for hours in front of a stunned crowd, how he ran out the door and how Alma of Alma's Restaurant sent a rescue party after him, how the villagers combed the forest with torches, how a woodcutter found Artie Shaw in a stand of pine and brought him back to life beside his fire.

But that was months ago, before the spring came. I am awake now, all alone, sitting in the cabin, looking out the window. The snow is melting outside. You can hear it: a trickle of water moving in the eaves. I've finished something. I feel calm. This thing is sitting here on the table, staring at me in silence: bright white pages with black specks, dirty snow. I don't know what this thing is, Betty, that I brought back with me from the other side, or what it means. All I know is that it is not a song.

ACKNOWLEDGMENTS

For a clear eye and unfailing patience in shepherding this collection into the world, deepest thanks are due to Callie Collins and Jill Meyers at A Strange Object.

Thanks, also, to the editors who first gave these stories homes: Michael Koch at *Epoch*; Hannah Tinti and Marie-Helene Bertino at *One Story*; T. Kira Madden at *No Tokens*; Natalie Eilbert and Dolan Morgan at *The Atlas Review*; J. T. Barbarese and Paul Lisicky at *StoryQuarterly*; Randy Rosenthal and Laura Mae Isaacman at *The Coffin Factory*; and Bradford Morrow at *Web Conjunctions*.

Thanks to the Kelly Writers House, for broadening my

horizons and exposing me to a series of escalating kitchen injuries; to my students, teachers, and colleagues at Temple University, who manage to fill such strangely shaped buildings with energy and spirit; and to Kevin James Holland, musical obsessive and maestro of Fiume, the best bar in Philadelphia.

To Alli Katz, for living with me, over and over.

Highest praises to the entire crew at Bluebond Guitars, who taught me more about songs than anyone, and especially the girls in Dad Likes Strawberry Jam; to Patrick at Brickbat Books, who sold me a literary education; and to the founders/proprietors/artists-in-residence at the building formerly known as Cha-Cha'razzi (a.k.a. Luigi Sammarone Off-Track Bedding), especially Rachael Cohen, Will Dean, Sarah Szymanski, Adriane Dalton, Nora Chase, Zach Fay, and Tristan Dahn, all of whom contributed to these stories in ways both visible and unseen.

For camaraderie and necessary talks in trying times, Ben Goldstein, Alyssa Songsiridej, Matt Jakubowski, Jacob Mazer, Jennifer Raphael, Hilary Plum, and Zach Savich.

For music making, mischief, and mutual appreciation, the inimitable Emily Bate and the greatness that is Adam Brody.

Endless gratitude to Dan Chaon, most generous man, who showed me what fiction was and how to write it. So many students owe you an enormous debt.

To Kate Johnson, my agent, first reader of these stories and trusted advisor in all matters, possessed of that rare combination of true faith and razor-sharp discernment—no thanks could be enough.

Much love to Mom, Dad, and Pam, for raising me to think of words as these magical things, and for keeping all these stories on the coffee table.

And to Larissa, best of all.

ABOUT THE AUTHOR

Sam Allingham grew up in rural New Jersey and Philadelphia. After graduating from Oberlin College, he worked for many years as a music teacher for adults and small(ish) children, before receiving an MFA from Temple University in 2013. His work has appeared in *One Story*, *American Short Fiction*, *Epoch*, *n+1*, *The Millions*, and *Full Stop*, among other publications. He currently lives in West Philadelphia and teaches at Temple University.

ABOUT A STRANGE OBJECT

Founded in 2012, A Strange Object is a women-run, fiction-focused press in Austin, Texas. The press champions debuts, daring writing, and good design across all platforms. Its titles are distributed by Small Press Distribution.